UNDONE!

ALSO BY PAUL JENNINGS

UNDONE!
More Mad Endings

Paul Jennings

VIKING

VIKING
Published by the Penguin Group
Penguin Books USA Inc., 375 Hudson Street, New York, New York 10014, U.S.A.
Penguin Books Ltd, 27 Wrights Lane, London W8 5TZ, England
Penguin Books Australia Ltd, Ringwood, Victoria, Australia
Penguin Books Canada Ltd, 10 Alcorn Avenue, Toronto, Ontario, Canada M4V 3B2
Penguin Books (N.Z.) Ltd, 182-190 Wairau Road, Auckland 10, New Zealand

Penguin Books Ltd, Registered Offices: Harmondsworth, Middlesex, England

First published in Australia by Penguin Books Australia, 1993
First published in the United States of America by Viking,
a division of Penguin Books USA Inc., 1995

3 5 7 9 10 8 6 4 2

CIP data is available upon request from the Library of Congress

ISBN 0-670-86005-0

Printed in U.S.A.
Set in Baskerville

For Sally

CONTENTS

BATTY

1

A stone with a hole in it. A sort of green-colored jewel in a leather pouch. Just lying there in the beam of my flashlight.

Someone must have dropped it. But who? There was only Dad and me and our two little tents, alone in the bush. I picked the pouch up by the piece of leather thong which was threaded through it. Then I crawled into my tent.

I should have shown Dad the stone with the hole in it. But he was snoring away inside his tent and I didn't want to wake him. And there was something odd about it. The pouch was worn and the thong was twisted. As if it had hung around someone's neck for many years.

Who was the owner? Who had lost it way out here in the wilderness?

I snuggled down inside my sleeping bag and hoped that no one was snooping around. The noises of the bush seemed especially loud. Frogs chirped in a billabong. "Well, *they* can't hurt you," I said softly.

Something bounded through the scrub. "Kangaroo," I whispered to myself.

A growling grunt filled the night air. "Koala," I thought hopefully.

I closed my eyes and tried to make sleep come. I dared not listen to the rustlings and sighings outside. I told myself that Dad's tent was only a few meters away. But in that dark, dark night it could have been a million miles.

Scared? I was terrified. What if someone was out there? Creeping. Watching. Waiting. "Get hold of yourself, girl," I said to myself. "There is no one out there."

A twig broke. Snapped clean in the night. I stopped breathing. I stopped moving. But I didn't stop thinking. "Go away. Please go away," begged my frozen brain. I wanted to call out to Dad but my mouth wouldn't work.

The flap of the tent lifted. I could see the stars and the black trees. Someone moved. A shadow rustling, searching. Hands took my bag and opened it. I wanted to cry out but something stopped me.

Two pinpoints of light moved in a dark head. Eyes. Desperate eyes.

Quietly I moved my fingers. Like a spider's legs they crept under the blankets toward my flashlight. "Softly, don't disturb him. Don't make him angry." With shaking hands I pointed the flashlight into the gloom. I felt like a soldier with an empty gun. I flicked on the switch.

And there he was. A wild boy with tangled hair and greasy skin. He was covered in flapping rags.

The tent was filled with a terrible squeaking like a million mice.

The boy reared back. In one hand he held a piece of cake from my bag. And in the other was the pouch with the hollow stone. He sucked in air with a hiss, turned to flee and then stopped.

He looked at me with a silent plea. A desperate call for help. He held his hand in front of his face to block out the glare of the flashlight. The moon escaped from a bank of clouds and softened the tent with light. I should have called for Dad. But my eyes were locked in silent conversation with the intruder.

I could see that the boy was as frightened as me. He was poised to run. Like a wild animal wanting food but unable to take it from a human hand. I had to be careful. A wrong movement and he . . .

"Hey," yelled Dad.

It was just as if someone had turned out a light. The boy vanished in a twinkle. I didn't even see him go.

2

Dad and I sat up nearly all night talking about what had happened.

It seems that a hermit called Lonely Pearson had once lived out here in a hut with his wife and son. The wife was an expert on bats, like Dad. Nine years ago she died and Lonely became enraged with grief.

Lonely did some mean things. He burned everything that belonged to her. Her books, her clothes, her photos of the bats. The lot. It was almost as if he was angry with her for dying and leaving him alone with his little five-year-old son—Philip.

The only thing that was left was a green stone with the hole in it. Philip's mother had always worn it around her neck. He used to play with it while she read him stories at bedtime.

After she died Philip hid the stone. Lonely Pearson ranted

and raved. He shouted and searched. He nearly tore their hut to pieces. But Philip wouldn't show him where it was. He closed his mouth and refused to speak. He kept his secret and Lonely never found the stone.

"So what happened to Philip?" I asked Dad.

"He ran off into the bush. Lonely couldn't find him. No one could find him. The police searched for weeks and weeks. Then they gave up. Everyone thought he was dead."

I took a deep breath. "What about Lonely?" I said.

"He spent every day searching for his son. He never gave up. Lonely died last year."

I couldn't stop thinking about that sad, bewildered face staring at me in the moonlight.

"How can he live out here?" I asked. "It gets really cold at night. And there's nothing to eat."

Dad shook his head and turned down the kerosene lamp. "That's enough for tonight," he said. "You go to sleep. We have two days of climbing before we reach the bat cave. You are going to need all the rest you can get."

"But . . ." I began.

"Good night, Rachel."

I heard him zip up his sleeping bag. I was in Dad's tent. It was a bit cramped but Dad thought it was safer.

"Good night," I mumbled. I was thinking about the next night. I was going back to my own tent. I had no doubts about that.

3

The next day was hot and our packs were heavy. Dad and I struggled through the dense bush. Down into wet gullies filled with tree ferns and leeches. Up dry, rocky slopes through sharp, scratching thorns. Along trails where kookaburras called and cicadas filled the air with chirping.

It was wonderful country but my pack was heavy. And so was my heart. There was a sadness in the air. At times I thought I glimpsed a hidden watcher. But I could never be quite sure. I would turn quickly. A branch moved slightly. Or did it?

We stopped for lunch in a mossy glen. Dad passed me a piece of cake. It was starting to go stale. I wrapped it up and put it in my pocket.

"Not hungry?" asked Dad.

"I'm keeping it for later," I replied. I was too. But not for me. I had plans for that bit of cake.

We packed up and moved on. Sometimes we went up. And sometimes down. But we were getting higher and higher.

My dad loved the outdoors. And of all living things he loved bats best. He was mad about them.

We were heading for a bat cave at the top of the mountain, Bat Peaks. Dad was going to block off the entrance to the cave. The roof was beginning to fall in. If it collapsed the whole colony of bats would be destroyed.

"But they will all starve," I had said when he first told me the plan.

"No," he had replied. "We block the cave entrance at night. When they are out feeding. They will be forced to find another cave. It's the only way to save the colony."

So there we were. Trudging up the mountain. On our way to blow up a bat cave before it collapsed and killed the bats.

Dad had bats on his brain. But all I could think of was a boy called Philip.

That night we camped in a forest clearing. Our campfire crackled between a circle of stones. Overhead the stars filled the cold night like a handful of sugar thrown at the sky. It didn't seem as if there could be anything wicked in the world.

The trees were ghostly and gray. The ground was home to pebbles and thorns and ants. I shuddered at the thought of someone living out there. Barefoot and alone.

Dad crawled into his tent. "Go to sleep, Rachel," he said.

"I'll just sit by the fire for a bit more," I told him.

You couldn't put much over on Dad. He knew what I was up to. "He won't come," he said. "He's wild and frightened. We'll call out a search party when we get back."

I sat there alone, but not alone, as the fire crackled and tossed sparks into the arms of the watching tree tops. The noises of the night kept me company.

I stared into the dark fringes of the forest. Watching for the watcher. Waiting for the waiter. Willing Philip to come.

At last the fire died and I shared the dark blanket of the night with the unseen creatures of the bush.

Quietly I walked to the edge of the forest and broke off a piece of cake. I placed it on a rock. A few meters away I did the same. I made a trail of cake leading to the edge of the dying fire.

Then I sat and waited.

Minutes passed. And hours. The moon slowly climbed behind the clouds. I struggled to keep my eyes open. But failed. You can only fight off sleep for so long. Then it wins and your head droops and your eyes close. That's what happened to me.

How long I dozed for I don't know. But something woke

me. Not a noise. Nothing from the forest. More like a thought or a dream. Or the memory of a woman's voice. I woke with a start and stared around the clearing. Something was different. Something was missing.

The first piece of cake. It was gone.

At that moment I half saw two things. High in a tree off to one side was a shadowy figure, watching from a branch. And on the edge of the clearing was someone else. I was sure it was Philip.

It was.

He cautiously crept forward into the open. Shadows fell across his body. He was still dressed like a beggar. Hundreds of flapping rags hung from his body.

The boy's eyes darted from side to side. He looked first at the cake and then at me. He crept forward a few steps and bent and picked up the cake. The moon slid out from its hiding place.

And Philip stood there, revealed. For a moment I couldn't take it in. Couldn't make sense of what my eyes were telling me. His rags flapped in the breeze. But the night was still and there was no breeze.

They were alive. His rags seethed and crawled and squeaked.

The wild boy was covered in bats. They hung from his arms and hair and chest. He was dressed in live bats. I couldn't believe it. Only his eyes were clear. His beautiful, dark eyes. I gave a scream and staggered backward.

5

The movement alarmed Philip and he threw his arms across his face. He was like a living book with its gray pages ruffling in a storm. Two bats flew up into the air and swooped under the trees.

Philip looked at me in fear and then up at the circling bats. Without a word he held his hands up to his mouth and started to whistle softly. The bats in the trees flew straight back and attached themselves to his hair. The others became calm.

"Sorry," I said in a hoarse voice. "I didn't mean to scare you." There were lots of things I wanted to say. My stomach felt strange. I could feel myself blushing. I wanted to say something tender. Something caring. Something that would make us friends. Or more than friends. But all I could think of saying was, "Have some cake."

Philip stared at me. And then at the cake. I could see that he wasn't sure. I wondered if he had ever seen a girl before.

"I'm your friend," I said. "I won't hurt you, I promise."

He was hungry. I guess that he hadn't tasted cake for a long, long time. Maybe he had been eating bat food. Fruit and moths and things.

He gave a sort of a smile. Only a small one. But it was enough to make my heart beat so fast that it hurt. Philip took a step toward the next piece of cake. He was starting to trust me. Maybe even to like me. As quick as a snake striking he pounced on the cake and began munching.

He ate like a five-year-old, shoving the cake in with both hands and smearing crumbs all over his face.

If only I could get him to trust me. I might be able to talk to him. To make him stay. He swallowed the last crumb and then just stood there staring into my eyes.

Slowly I took a step forward. "It's okay," I whispered. "It's okay."

The bats murmured and fluttered. He was ready to run.

But he let me approach. An invisible bond was holding us together.

"Aagh . . ." There was a terrible scream from the treetops. A branch broke with a crack. The shadowy figure I'd seen plunged down, grabbing at branches and yelling. He landed with a thump and lay there groaning. It was Dad.

The bats scattered into the air like a swarm of huge bees. Philip's cloak was gone. He stood there, naked. He glared at me. He thought we had tried to trap him. He raised his fist and then, thinking better of it, fled into the forest.

"Come back," I yelled. Tears flooded down my face. "Please come back."

But only the bats stayed, circling above me, squeaking in fright.

I ran over to Dad. "Sorry," he said. "I couldn't let you meet him alone. I had to keep an eye on you."

"Are you okay?" I asked.

Dad tried to stand but he couldn't. "Sprained ankle," he groaned.

We both looked up at the circling cloud of bats. They didn't seem to know where to go. A sound drifted on the night air. "Sh . . ." said Dad.

A soft, squeaking whistle pierced the night. It was the whistling noise Philip made through his fingers. The bats squeaked frantically, circled once and flew off after the sound. Dad and I were alone in the dark, silent clearing.

Frenzied thoughts filled my mind. Philip, Philip. We have
betrayed you. Dad, how could you spy on me? Dad, are you
hurt?

Dad was groaning and holding his ankle. "That's the end
of the expedition," he said. "I can't walk a step."

"But what about the bats? The cave might fall on them.
The whole colony will die unless we blow up the cave."

"I'm sorry, Rachel," said Dad. "I can't move. And you can't
go alone. We'll stay here. The rangers know our route. They'll
send a helicopter when we don't arrive back on time. We'll
be safe if we stay here."

I took a deep breath. "But that's in three days. What if the
cave collapses? I'm going on my own."

"Don't be silly," said Dad. "You've never even seen a stick
of dynamite. I wouldn't let you anywhere near it. You'd kill
yourself." He grabbed his pack and held it tight. The dynamite
was inside.

"There's something you haven't thought of," I said.
"Yes?"
"Philip. He is covered in bats. He wears them like clothes."
"So?" said Dad.
"And he whistles through his fingers and calls them."
"Yes?"
"Where do you think he lives? He is a bat boy. He must live
in that cave with the bats. And the roof is about to fall in. We
have to save him."

Dad didn't say anything for quite a while. He knew I was
right.

"You're not going anywhere," he said at last. "You might
get lost. You can't handle dynamite. The boy won't come out

of the cave anyway. He's a wild thing. He hasn't spoken to anyone since he was five. No. We wait here until help arrives. And that's the end of it."

When your father says, "That's the end of it," it usually is. But not this time.

I don't know how to say it. But I couldn't get Philip's face out of my mind. My stomach was churning. My face was hot. Just thinking about him gave me the shivers. That cave might fall in at any minute. He could die alone, covered in bats. Far from his people. In nine years he had never felt the touch of a woman's hand.

"I'm going," I said. "And you can't stop me."

"No," Dad said with an iron face. "You're only fourteen. I forbid it."

"You've got a sprained ankle and can't move," I said. "You can't forbid anything. Good-bye." I just turned around and started walking out of the clearing into the night forest.

"All right. All right, Rachel," he called. "But come back. You have to prepare. Take food and a compass. Ropes. Everything. Otherwise there will be two dead teenagers."

So that's what happened. I packed my knapsack with food and everything I might need. Except the dynamite. There was no way Dad would even take his hand off it.

By morning I was ready to leave. I headed off in the direction of Bat Peaks. The mountain loomed above us like a pair of giant wings. "Remember," yelled Dad. "Don't go inside the cave. Promise."

"Yes," I said as I pushed into the bush. "I promise."

It was tough going. The higher I went the more difficult it became. The trees gave way to giant boulders and scrub. My knees were raw and bleeding. My feet were sore.

But I didn't care. I had to get Philip and the bats out of that cave. But how?

I held my fingers up to my lips and blew. Nothing except a rush of hot air. Not so much as a squeak. If I could learn to whistle through my fingers I might be able to call him. And bring out the bats.

But I just couldn't get the hang of it. I always admired those kids at school who could whistle through their fingers.

The sun rose high above me and then began to lower itself toward the rim of the mountains. Before I knew it, the sky was growing dark.

I was perched high above the forest on a mountain ledge. The trees below looked like the surface of an ocean gently rippling in the last of the sunlight. Cockatoos circled, screeching above their roosts. I jiggled down into my sleeping bag and hoped that I wouldn't roll over the edge in my sleep.

Not that I did sleep. The ground was hard. And I couldn't stop thinking about Philip.

So I practiced finger whistling. I blew until my lips were parched and dry. But not a sound could I get. It was hopeless.

The next day I scrambled up and on. Rocks tumbled and crashed under my feet. They bounded into the valley way below. I became reckless. I didn't stop to rest.

I knew that time was passing too quickly. I dreaded to think what I might find when I reached the bat cave.

I stopped for nothing. Not even to use the compass. After all, there was only one way to go. Up.

That's how I became lost. Found myself on a rocky outcrop. Tumbled into a crevasse. Lay dazed for hours. Lost my pack. Lost my compass. Lost my senses.

In the end I crawled out and sat and cried. I had no map. No way of knowing where I was. Or where the cave was. I was totally lost.

That's when I saw it. Just hanging there on a bramble. A leather pouch. I stumbled over and grabbed it. I fumbled with the catch and looked inside: the green-colored stone with a hole in it.

Philip must have dropped it again. Twice in three days?

I couldn't believe that he would keep dropping something so precious. It was the only thing he had to remind him of his mother.

I smiled. I told myself that he left it there on purpose. For me. To show me the way. That's what I thought anyway. That's what I hoped.

I grabbed the pouch and stumbled on. On to the very top. On to where the sheer rock cliffs fell down on every side.

A small bridge of rock spanned a drop into the valley miles below. It was so far down that my head swam.

And there, on the other side, hanging under an enormous ledge, was what I had come for. The bat cave.

Normally I would not have crossed that rocky bridge. Not for anything.

But somehow I forced my trembling legs over. Until I stood there peering at the cave, staring into its black jaws.

All was silent except for the soft breath of the cold mountain breeze.

I looked at the roof of the cave. It seemed okay to me. How did Dad know that it was going to fall in?

I held my fingers to my mouth and blew. Nothing. I couldn't get a whistle. Not a squeak. It was hopeless.

"Philip," I called. "Philip, come out. The cave is going to collapse."

Silence was the only reply.

I forgot my promise to Dad. Or I pushed it into the back of my mind. I'm not sure which.

With thumping heart I made my way into the gloom. Water pinged in the distance. A soft burbling noise surrounded me.

As my eyes became used to the dark I could make out a huge boulder in the roof. It seemed to move. It did move. It was covered in thousands of hanging bats. Their wings rippled like a blanket floating on a lake.

How long before that rock would fall? I trembled. "Philip," I called urgently. "Philip."

No answer. I raised my voice. "Come out, you stupid boy," I shouted. "Come out."

It was not Philip who was stupid. It was me. My voice echoed terribly around the walls. It bounced off the rocks. It shook the dry air.

Without a speck of warning the living boulder above plunged to the ground. It shook the mountain to its roots. It filled the cave with choking dust.

My voice had dislodged the boulder.

Thousands of bats mingled with the dust. Circling, screaming. Screeching. I turned and fled into the glaring sunlight. Another boulder fell. The sound of its smash pummeled the walls. More rocks fell.

"Philip," I screamed. "Philip, come out."

Dust, like smoke from a fallen chimney, billowed into the mountain air. And through it came Philip. Blood flowed from a deep wound in his head. He staggered out and fell at my feet. Unconscious.

I dragged him clear of the mouth of the cave. I pulled him toward the rocky bridge. And then stopped and stared, filled with terror at the sight.

The bridge had broken. Fallen into the valley below. We were trapped on the mountaintop. There was no way back.

8

Naked. Not a stitch on.

Poor Philip. Lying there on the bare mountain. Exposed to the wind. Was he dead? I didn't know.

I should have put my sweater over him. Covered his nakedness. But there wasn't time. Rocks were still falling. There was no way down. And the bats. The bats were doomed. "Help. Someone help."

No one answered. I was alone.

I held my fists up to my mouth and blew. I wanted so badly to save the bats. I tried to whistle loudly but nothing came.

The bats were still in there. They would die because of me. Because I raised my voice and disturbed the rocks. And Philip. Would he die too?

He opened his eyes. He looked at me. Was he accusing me? Did his eyes say that I had murdered his friends?

No, they did not. He smiled. He tried to speak but he couldn't. Instead he touched the pouch that hung around my neck. His mother's stone.

"This," I said. He nodded and once more closed his eyes.

I took out the green stone and stared at it. I knew what to do.

I began to blow through the hole.

The air was filled with a whistle. A strong, clear squeaking. The most beautiful sound I had ever heard.

The cave echoed thunder. Not of falling rocks but of beating wings. Hundreds, thousands, millions of wings. The bats surged out of the cave. They darkened the sky. They filled the mountaintop until nothing could be seen but a swirling swarm of gray. I had saved the colony.

Philip opened his eyes and smiled. He took the stone from my fingers and blew. He whistled his own message to the bats.

They dropped out of the sky like autumn leaves in a storm. I shrieked. They grabbed my hair. My feet. They pierced my sweater with tiny claws. The bats hung from me like rags.

I stared at Philip. He was no longer naked, but like me wore a living cloak. Bat boy. Bat girl. Stranded. Together on Bat Peaks.

The bats beat their wings in a terrible rhythm. They stirred up a storm of squealing fury.

My feet left the ground. I was flying. Carried up, up, up. Lifted into the sky by a flurry of flapping wings. Held by tiny feet.

The mountain lay far beneath. I saw an explosion of dust spurt out from the cave below. The roof had caved in.

I gasped in shock at the sight of the valleys below. Like the prey of a mountain eagle I was lifted between the mountaintops.

And above me, Philip, carried by his coat of friends, soared and swooped in the empty sky.

He waved and pointed.

16

Far, far beneath, in the tangled mat of trees was a wisp of smoke. Dad's campfire.

The bats began to descend. Taking us down through the biting air.

For the first time Philip spoke. He pointed down at the campfire and said just one word.

"Home."

And that is where we went.

MOONIES

I, Adam Hill, agree to stand
on the Wollaston Bridge at four
o'clock and pull down my pants.
I will then flash a moonie at
Mr. Bellow, the school principal.

Who would be mad enough to sign such a thing? Suicide—
flashing a bare bottom at Mr. Bellow.

1

I'm going to explain what happened on the Wollaston Bridge.
Then you will know the worst thing that has ever happened
to me.

Normally I would never have agreed to sign the contract.
Not in a million years. But I did. And do you know why?
Well, I'll tell you, even though it's embarrassing. Even though
it is something I'd rather not talk about.

The truth of the matter is: I couldn't read. I didn't know
what I was signing.

I couldn't write. I couldn't spell. And I couldn't tell anyone.

Not being able to read was a big problem. I used to get into that much hot water over it.

Like, for example, when I ordered food at the coffee shop. I would look up at the prices but didn't know what to order. Did it say, "Hamburger with the lot"? Or did it say, "No checks accepted"?

Once I pointed at the sign and said, "One of those, please, with catsup."

The woman who was serving stared at me for quite a while. Then she said, "You'll find the ladies restroom is a bit tough, love. Especially with catsup." Everyone in the shop laughed. I ran out with tears in my eyes. It was no joke, I can tell you.

After that I worked out a new approach. I would listen to what the person in front of me asked for. If they said, "One piece of grilled fish with fries," I would say, "Same again."

Or they might ask for, "A dollar of fries and two potato cakes."

When it was my turn I would pipe up, "Same again."

That worked well because I always knew what I was going to get.

The only trouble was that I wasn't listening properly one day. I didn't hear what the guy in front of me ordered. "Same again," I said.

The girl handed me fifteen cheeseburgers. And I had to take them. It cost me a month's allowance. I still can't look at a cheeseburger. You don't feel too good after eating fifteen of them.

Anyway, not being able to read and write was the pits. Especially when I started a new school.

"I'll write a note to the teachers," said Dad. "Then they'll give you special help with your reading. There's nothing wrong with that."

"No," I said. "I don't want anyone at this school to know."

Dad looked sad. "Adam," he said. "You have to face up to it, not hide it. You're no good at reading but you can do other things. You're about the best drawer I've ever seen. Most people can't draw for nuts. Everybody's good at different things. You're good at painting and drawing."

"Give me a week," I said. "Just one week at the new school before you tell them I can't read."

He didn't want to do it. But in the end he agreed. My dad is the greatest bloke around. The best. "Okay," he said. "But look, why don't you take one of your paintings? On the first day. Show them how good you are. Take that one of the wallaby."

2

So there I was on the first day at the new school. Shaking at the knees.

Right away I found out two things—one good and one bad. I'll give you the bad first.

There was a bully at the school. Isn't there always? His name was Kevin Grunt but everyone just called him Grunt. He was big and tough and had a long nose.

It was almost as if he had been waiting for me. He took one look at me and then marched across the classroom. He whacked this piece of paper down on the desk. "New kids have to prove themselves," he said. "Sign here. It's a contract."

I went red in the face. Not because I didn't want to prove myself. No, not that. But because I didn't want anyone to know that I couldn't read. I had no idea what was written on that bit of paper.

I gave a little grin and held up my bandaged arm. "Can't write," I said.

I always used to put my left arm in a sling when there was going to be writing to do. That way no one would be able to know I couldn't spell. Easy. It never failed.

Except this time.

"Just write your name with your right hand, idiot," said Grunt. "Put a cross if you like."

I looked at the piece of paper. Then I stared up at the faces that surrounded me. The whole class was waiting to see what I would do. I wanted to say, "Will someone read it out, please?"

But of course I couldn't say that. They would all know my terrible secret. So I picked up the pen and scribbled my name with my right hand.

A kid with red hair and freckles pushed through to the front. "I think it's mean," he said. "He's only a new kid. Give him a break, Grunt."

"Shut up, Blue," said Grunt. "Unless you want to take his place."

That's how I became friends with Blue.

"You're mad," he said. "You have to go out on Wollaston Bridge. At four o'clock. And flash your behind at Mr. Bellow. There's nowhere for you to run or hide. You'll be in the middle of the bridge all alone. You'll get caught for sure."

I smiled weakly. "I could just go home," I said.

Blue shook his head. "Grunt and his mates will never leave you alone if you break your contract. Not now that you've signed. You have to do it."

And the good thing? What was the good thing that happened?

Well, they were having this competition in Melbourne at the National Gallery. An exhibition. One person from each school could submit a piece of art.

Before the first period was over I found myself in Mr. Bellow's office. He stood there looking at my painting of the wallaby. He shook his head. "Fantastic," he said. "I can't believe that you are only thirteen. The gallery director is coming tomorrow. I'm sure that she will pick this. It's terrific. We're very glad to have such a talent at our school."

I was rapt. Maybe I would become famous. More than anything in the world I wanted to be a painter. I was never happier than when I had a brush in my hand.

I would have been the happiest person in the world—if I didn't have to go onto the Wollaston Bridge after school. And flash my bare behind at Mr. Bellow.

To be honest, I am a shy person. I didn't want anyone to see my bottom. Oh, oh, oh. What a terrible thing. I just couldn't do it. But I couldn't *not* do it either. Could I? Not after I had signed a contract.

3

The whole school turned out to see the sight: girls, boys, little kids, big kids. The lot. They hid in the grass. Climbed trees. Every hiding place was taken. No one wanted to be seen by Mr. Bellow.

So there I was. In the middle of the bridge. Kevin Grunt was clever. He had made sure that there was no hiding place for me. Mr. Bellow would see my lonely bottom. Then he would see my face. And I would be dead meat.

Oh, the shame. Oh, the misery. The bushes were filled with

giggling and laughing. What could I do? How could I get out of it? I didn't want anyone to see my behind. Bottoms are very personal things.

My knees were knocking. I felt like crying. I couldn't chicken out. Not with the whole school watching.

I looked along the road. A car was coming. It was Mr. Bellow's Falcon. Oh no. Help. Please. Please. I can't do it.

I undid my belt. I fumbled with my top button.

The car was coming closer. My fingers were like jelly. I couldn't get my zipper down.

Mr. Bellow was so close that I could see his bushy eyebrows.

I pulled down my jeans. And my underpants. I was undone. My skinny backside was there for all to see.

With gritted teeth and closed eyes I turned and stuck my bare bottom up into the air.

There was a squeal of brakes. The car stopped. There was dead silence on the bridge. I dared not breathe. I tried to pull up my pants. But I was frozen with fear. I just stood there like a man before a firing squad.

Hopeless. Jeansless. Defenseless.

Mr. Bellow stood there shaking. He was snorting through his nostrils like a horse. I have never seen anyone so angry in all my life.

He only said two words. But they were terrible words. They were words that spelled doom.

"Adam Hill," he spat out.

Mr. Bellow jumped back into the car and drove off. I knew that tomorrow would be the end of the world. Mr. Bellow knew who I was. There was no doubt about that.

The funny thing is that the kids didn't laugh much. I pulled up my pants and started to walk off the bridge.

Blue rushed up and put his arm around me.

"Good for you, Adam," yelled out a girl with black hair.

"Good one, Hill," someone else called out.

Quite a few kids came up and patted me on the back. They were all glad that it wasn't them who'd had to do it.

Kevin Grunt didn't like all this. Not one little bit.

"Pathetic," was all he said. Then he and his pals headed off down the road.

I was glad that it was over.

Except that it wasn't all over. Not by a long way. In the morning I would have to go to the office for sure. Mr. Bellow might kick me out of school. What if he called the police? Baring your behind could even be against the law.

When all the kids had gone I took off my bandage and headed home.

"How did your first day go?" asked Dad.

I smiled weakly. I couldn't tell him what I had done. He would be so ashamed. "Er, I think my painting of the wallaby is going to be shown in the National Gallery," I said.

"Wonderful," yelled Dad. "Well done, Adam. I am so proud of you."

That night I couldn't sleep. I just worried and worried. What if it got in the newspaper? What if the whole world found out what I had done? What was Mr. Bellow going to do?

I tried to think of the worst punishment. Saturday morning detention. Expelled. Told off in front of the whole school. Mr. Bellow complaining to Dad. The police brought into it.

But it was none of those. It was something worse.

I stood in Mr. Bellow's office and stared at the carpet.

"This afternoon," said Mr. Bellow, "the director of the National Gallery will be coming to see if we have a painting for the exhibition. We won't. We are not going to be represented by a boy who disgraces the school by revealing his private parts."

He handed me back the painting of the wallaby.

My heart sank. Oh no. This was the very worst. I wanted everyone to see my painting. I wanted Dad to be proud. I wanted to be good at something. Before all the kids found out that I couldn't read.

I trudged back to class. Tears were running down my cheeks. I tried to wipe them off but I didn't have a tissue. I hoped that the kids wouldn't see I had been bawling.

5

When I got back to class there was no teacher there.

"The poor little wimp has been crying," jeered Kevin Grunt.

I looked at him. I couldn't stand it anymore. From somewhere deep inside I found a little speck of courage. "You're a coward," I yelled. "You wouldn't have the guts to do what I did."

Grunt looked around the class with a fierce expression.

"Yeah," said Blue. "You wouldn't do it."

A few other kids joined in. "Yeah," they said. "Let's see *you* flash a moonie, Grunt."

"Okay," said Kevin Grunt. "Just watch me."

He grabbed a bit of paper and started to scribble on it.

"This is another contract," he said. "I'll flash a moonie myself. See if I don't."

I looked at it. I could make out a few words but most of it was just scribble to me. I pulled out the first contract and compared them. This one looked just the same. But I couldn't be sure.

"We'll both sign it," he said. He put his name on the bottom and held it out for me. I was in a spot. I couldn't very well ask him to read it out. But I had to do something.

"I have one extra requirement," I said.

Everyone looked at me. I tried to think of something. Anything.

"I get to paint a picture on your behind first."

A great howl of laughter went up. "No way," yelled Kevin Grunt.

"Chicken," said Blue.

I thought that Grunt's face was going to fall off. He just couldn't take being called a chicken. He grabbed the paper and wrote an extra bit on the bottom. Then we both signed it. "See ya after school, wimp," said Grunt.

Just then the teacher came in and everyone scurried back to their seats.

At recess I told Blue that I couldn't read. He was good about it really. He didn't care at all and promised to keep my secret. He read the contract out to me.

"One word is different," I said.

Blue nodded. "It says Wollaston *Road,* not Wollaston *Bridge.* He's going to hide in the bushes and stick his behind out. Then he will run off into the trees and Mr. Bellow won't know who did it. He might even think it is you doing it again."

"Oh no," I groaned. "I didn't think of that. I'll get the blame and Kevin Grunt will get off scot free."

Blue was really glum. I could see that he thought I had been sucked in. "And why did you say you wanted to paint his behind? What are you going to paint?"

"A wallaby," I said. "I'm good at wallabies."

Blue looked at me as if I was crazy. "If you paint a wallaby Mr. Bellow will be sure it's your bum. He's already seen your painting."

My heart sank. I sure was dumb. I was in trouble with Mr. Bellow. Dad would find out for sure. And I had missed out on my chance to have my painting in the National Gallery. And now Mr. Bellow would see Grunt's painted bottom and think I was flashing a moonie again.

I felt like screaming. But there was nothing I could do.

6

Everything happened just like I hoped it wouldn't.

There was Grunt. On Wollaston Road. He had picked out a nice little hole in some bushes. He was going to poke his bare behind out through it. Then he was going to run away unseen. And I was going to get the blame because one of my paintings would be there for Mr. Bellow to see.

"Er, it's all right about the painting. I don't need to do it," I said.

But Grunt was too smart for me. He had already figured out that I would get the blame. He even brought his own box of paints with him. "Get on with it, Hill," he said. "It's in the contract."

Well, all the kids were there. I had no choice.

Grunt dropped his pants and I started to paint away with my left hand. I couldn't think of what to do. "Hurry up," growled Kevin Grunt. "He'll be here soon." Grunt was having the time of his life. He knew that he'd tricked me again.

I had just finished putting the last dab of paint on when a car approached. Mr. Bellow's Falcon.

We all ran and hid. Kevin Grunt stuck his behind out through the hole in the bushes. I closed my eyes and held my breath.

There was a squeal of brakes. A car door opened. Mr. Bellow jumped out. So did someone else. There was a passenger in the car.

Grunt ran for it. He pulled up his pants and shot off into the scrub. There was no way that Mr. Bellow would have seen who it was.

Mr. Bellow stood there shaking. He was snorting through his nostrils like a horse. I have never seen anyone so angry in all my life.

He only said two words. But they were terrible words. They were words that spelled doom.

"Kevin Grunt," he spat out.

Mr. Bellow jumped back into the car and drove off. I knew that tomorrow would be the end of the world. For Kevin Grunt. Mr. Bellow knew who he was. There was no doubt about that.

7

Well, Grunt really got it. He was given three Saturday morning detentions. And no one was sorry. Not one single person.

Still and all, his punishment wasn't as bad as mine. I had missed out on having a painting in the National Gallery.

That night I was pretty miserable. Until the phone rang. "For you," said Dad.

"Yes?" I said into the phone.

I listened. I listened real good. It was the director of the National Gallery.

"I was traveling home with Mr. Bellow today," she said. "And a painting stared out at me from the bushes. An unusual painting. I believe you were the artist. A left-hander they tell me."

"Yes," I mumbled.

"It was wonderful," said the director. "I want you to give us something to put in the gallery."

Well, talk about rapt. Dad was so proud. He went out and bought me a book about this painter Van Gogh who cut his own ear off. The words were hard to read. But it was so interesting that I started to get the hang of it. I just had to find out what happened in the end.

Blue was proud of me too. "You're a genius, Adam," he said. "But you're lucky. How did Mr. Bellow know that it was Grunt's bare bottom? And what did you paint on it anyway?"

Blue laughed when he heard my answer.

"I painted a face," I said. "One with a long nose. I think Mr. Bellow recognized who it was right away."

NOSEWEED

Think of honey.
Think of rotten, stinking fish.
Put them together and what have you got?
DISGUSTING COD-LIVER OIL.
That's what.

1

The nonsense you have just read was not written by me. My grandson Anthony wrote it. Silly boy.

I love cod-liver oil. I have been eating it for ninety-five years. It is good for you. It is delicious. In fact I would probably have died when I was only eighty if it weren't for my daily dose of cod-liver oil. Wonderful stuff. Full of natural flavor and vitamins.

Just because I am an old man doesn't mean that I don't know anything. But Anthony won't take any notice. He only eats what he likes. Chocolates, hamburgers, ice cream. Rubbish like that. Bad for you.

We are great pals. We love each other—Anthony and I. We see eye to eye on everything. Except food.

Anthony has been coming to my house every Christmas since he was born. He loves it. But not at meal times.

I remember when he was only three. Everyone was there at the table. Gran was alive at the time, bless her heart.

I put Anthony's plate of vegetable mush in front of him. He closed his mouth and shook his head. He didn't want vegetable mush. Not even after I had grown the carrots and brussels sprouts in my own backyard. The best carrots in town. I've won prizes for those carrots.

And the little beggar wouldn't eat them. What a nerve. It made my blood boil, I can tell you. He wanted roast beef and plum pudding like the rest of us. And he was only three.

I looked across the table at him. Then I pounced and put him in a headlock. I forced open his jaw. I shoved a spoonful of vegetable mush between his lips and clamped his mouth shut. "Gotcha," I yelled.

"Let him go, dear," said Gran, bless her heart. "He's only three."

"Never," I said. "Not until he eats his vegetable mush."

Anthony never said a thing. Not that he could talk, what with me holding him in a headlock. But he didn't fight. He didn't squirm. He didn't make a sound. He is a stubborn kid. Takes after his Gran, bless her heart.

So that is how it went. I ate my soup with my left hand and kept Anthony in the headlock with my right one. "Give in," I said.

No answer. He didn't even shake his head. Not that he could even if he had wanted to.

Next we had the roast beef. I had to ask Gran (bless her heart) to cut mine up so I could eat with one hand. It took me fifty minutes but I managed it.

"Give in," I said.

Anthony didn't even blink. He just stared in front of him with a stubborn look in his eyes.

Now I had a problem. Was the vegetable mush still in there? Or had he swallowed it? I dared not let go.

Gran served up the plum pudding, bless her heart. It was delicious. Custard and cream too. Easy to eat with one hand.

I kept the headlock on Anthony. "Have you swallowed your vegetable mush?" I said. "If you have I'll let you go."

No answer. So I didn't let him go.

We had coffee. We had jam tarts. But still Anthony kept his mouth clamped closed. Or I should say *I* kept it clamped closed.

Everyone left the table except Anthony and me. Hours passed. The afternoon drifted into the evening. But still he wouldn't budge. So we just sat there. Him in his highchair and me putting on the stranglehold.

He must have swallowed it, I thought. My arm was getting pins and needles. I couldn't last any longer. So I let go.

Anthony spat the vegetable mush out onto the table.

Disgusting.

2

So that is how it is every Christmas when Anthony comes to stay. We have hassles over his food. And now he won't take his cod-liver oil. Even though he is thirteen years old.

Take this year, for example.

I was out in the hothouse when he arrived. I was trying to cross a Granny Smith apple with a Golden Delicious. I wanted to invent a new type of apple. A Golden Gran. Named after Gran. Bless her heart.

Excuse me a minute. A tear is rolling down my cheek. I always start to cry a bit when I think of her. Now she is dead and all. It's lonely without Gran. We were married for sixty years.

Now there is just me. And old Cameo, my horse. I love Cameo but she's not much company. Horses can love you but they can't talk.

She loves apples, does Cameo. She trots across the garden and pinches one out of your hand if you don't watch out.

I was mad about apples, too. If I could name a new type of apple after Gran, her memory would live forever. That's what I wanted to do. I would call it Golden Gran. Just think of it.

But it never worked. I just couldn't manage to develop a new type no matter how hard I tried.

Anyway, Anthony walked in while I was trying to fertilize my new species. "Grandpa," he said. "I am happy to be here. I am glad to see you again." He planted a kiss on my wrinkled old face. Then he said, "But I am not having cod-liver oil this year. I am too old for it. And I hate the stuff. It makes me spew."

I didn't say anything. I just made my plans. I would get it into him somehow. For his own sake.

Well, the next morning I put some cod-liver oil on a spoon. Lovely, like honey it is. With a smooth fish taste. Then I dipped it in my homemade granola: nuts, seeds, fruit, dried veggies. A wonderful mixture.

"Here," I said. "I've blended it with my special granola. Delicious."

Anthony shook his head. Stubborn boy.

"If you want the money for the movies today," I said, "you have to eat your granola and cod-liver oil."

"Blackmail," said Anthony.

"It's for your own good," I said.

To my great surprise he just nodded and opened his mouth. But I knew what he was up to. I was a kid myself once. He couldn't fool me. He was going to go outside and spit it out. I wasn't born yesterday.

"Promise me you won't spit it out," I said.

He looked at me for ages without answering. "Okay," he said at last.

I gave him the spoon and he put the granola and cod-liver oil into his mouth. His eyes started to water. His face went red. He held his hands up to his mouth and rushed over to the sink.

"You promised," I yelled.

He looked at me with staring eyes. Anyone would think I had pulled his fingernails out. It was only granola and cod-liver oil, for goodness sake. What a fuss over nothing.

"Swallow," I said. "Get it over and done with."

Anthony grabbed a piece of paper. He scribbled a message.

DISGUSTING. I CAN'T GET IT DOWN. I'LL BE SICK.

I took out my wallet and gave him ten dollars. "Here's the money for the movies," I said. "I've kept my word, now you keep yours. You promised not to spit it out."

His eyes were still watering. He had the granola and cod-liver oil in his mouth. He just wouldn't swallow it. Talk about stubborn. He snatched the ten-dollar bill and headed for the door. His cheeks were bulging out like two balloons.

"No you don't," I said. "You're going to spit it out on the way. I'm coming too. To keep an eye on you."

I grabbed my walking stick and hat and hobbled after him.

Down the street he went with me following. He stopped at the bus stop. "Mmnn, mnn, mng, mng," he said.

I couldn't understand a word. I think he said something like, "Please go home, Gramps, it's embarrassing."

Funny that. How kids get embarrassed by adults. I don't think he liked me being with him in my old gardening boots.

"No way," I said. "I'm staying until you swallow."

Lucky I did too. He never would have survived without me.

The bus pulled up and we got on. Of course Anthony couldn't talk. "Where to?" asked the bus driver.

"Mmm, nn, mng," said Anthony.

The bus driver looked at him as if he was crazy. "Knox City Shopping Center," I said. "One and a half, please."

We sat down and the bus started off. Passengers were staring at us. They were kindly old folk like me. Anthony was going red in the face. Kids get embarrassed about anything these days. He was ashamed of me. His own flesh and blood.

"Won't swallow his cod-liver oil." I said in a loud voice. "So I'm making sure he doesn't spit it out."

The passengers nodded. "Kids these days are spoiled," said an elderly lady.

Everyone oohed and aahed. They were all on my side. "My mother couldn't even afford cod-liver oil," said a bald man in the back.

"Yes," said a mother with two children on her knee. "Stick with the little rascal. Don't let him win. Make him swallow it."

I grinned. I knew I was right. Kids need discipline. There was no way I was going to let him spit out that granola and cod-liver oil.

And if he was embarrassed having his grandpa around, too bad.

35

3

Anthony jumped off the bus at Knox City. He tried to lose me in the crowd. Up the escalator, down the elevator. In one door, out of another. But I was too quick for him. He just couldn't shake me off.

Finally he went up to the box office at the cinema. "Which show, love?" said the lady ticket seller.

"Mnn, mmn, mng," he said.

"*Fairies in the Dell,*" I said. "One and a half, please."

"Mmnn, mmnng," Anthony was shaking his head. He didn't want to see *Fairies in the Dell.* He pointed to a sign that said *Blood of the Devil.*

The ticket seller gave him a ticket and Anthony rushed off. I quickly bought a ticket and followed. *Blood of the Devil.* That was no show for a child.

I hobbled after him into the dark cinema. It was all I could do to find him. I plonked myself down in the next seat. It was so dark that I could hardly see. I had to make sure that he didn't spit the cod-liver oil under the seat.

I didn't look at the screen. I just kept staring at Anthony's lips. My eyes became used to the dark and I could see that his cheeks were still swollen with the granola and cod-liver oil.

On the screen, worms were coming out of a grave. It was a terrible movie. Disgusting.

Just then something happened. Something that I found hard to believe. Something that you will find hard to believe. A little tubular shape like a worm wriggled out between Anthony's lips.

"Aagh," I screamed. "A worm."

"Shhh," said someone behind.

"Quiet," barked another voice. "If you're frightened, don't go to horror movies."

"Quick, Anthony," I whispered fiercely. "Spit it out. It's okay about the cod-liver oil. Spit it out."

The worm thing was wriggling farther and farther out of his mouth. It sort of snaked its way up past Anthony's eye.

He shook his head. Talk about stubborn. It was just like when he was three. Once he made up his mind, that was it.

The worm thing grew longer and longer. It oozed out of his mouth and wrapped itself around his head. What could it be? Terrible, terrible.

"Spit," I yelled. "For heaven's sake, Anthony. Spit."

"Shut up, you old fool," said a voice behind us in the darkness.

I had to save Anthony. Had to get this wretched thing out of the boy's mouth. I reached up and touched the writhing worm.

It wasn't a worm. It was a plant. A long tendril grew out of his mouth and twirled around his head.

My mind started to spin. What had I done to the poor boy? What was going on?

And then I realized.

The granola was growing. One of the seeds had sprouted in the cod-liver oil. It was growing so fast that I could see it move. Like a snake stretching itself. Out and around.

Then something else happened. Two more shoots erupted. One out of each nostril. It looked as if he needed to wipe his nose. Badly.

"Spit it out, Anthony," I shrieked. "For heaven's sake, boy, you've got a noseweed."

Growls and loud whispers came from the audience around.

"Shut up, pops."

"Get the manager."

"Chuck the old fool out."

Anthony just sat there staring at the screen. He didn't even care that the granola in his mouth was growing. Nothing would make him open his mouth. He was teaching me a lesson. He was as stubborn as Gran, bless her heart. If only she were here. She would know what to do.

"Come on, boy. Let's go," I said.

Anthony shook his head. I tried to pull him out of his seat but he was too strong.

"Shut up," came a voice.

"Keep still," said another.

I let go. If I made any more fuss they would kick me out of the place. I buried my head in my hands and closed my eyes. I just couldn't look at Anthony's sprouting mouth.

The other people settled down for a bit. I kept my eyes closed and sat still. No one complained. Not at first anyway.

Suddenly a voice said, "Take off that hat."

"Yes, we can't see."

"What a nerve, wearing a hat like that at the movies."

"I'm getting the manager."

I opened my eyes and screamed. Anthony's head was covered in branches and leaves. Stems snaked out of his mouth and nose and twisted upward. Instead of hair, he had a mass of leaves wrapped around his skull. He looked like he was wearing a ridiculous hat made of bushes. The people behind couldn't see the screen.

Just then a man with a flashlight came down the aisle. It was the manager. He grabbed me firmly by the arm. "Come with me, you two," he said. "You can't carry on like that in here."

He led us both down the dark aisle and out into the bright light of the lobby.

4

The manager glared at Anthony. "Very funny," he said. "Dressing up like that and spoiling the movie for everyone else."

"He's not dressing up," I gasped. "It's growing out of his mouth. Granola and cod-liver oil."

The manager shook his head at me angrily. "Practical jokes. At your age you should know better." He turned around and stomped off.

"Spit," I said to Anthony. "Get rid of it. Quick."

He just shook his head. He was still trying to teach me a lesson. And it was working.

"We're going home," I said. I grabbed his hand and pulled him through the crowds. More leaves and twigs were growing in front of my eyes. And Anthony's eyes too. I couldn't even see his face anymore.

A crowd of little kids and their mothers started to follow us.

"Look at that, Mum."

"How do they do it?"

"It's one of those in-store promotions, dear. It's probably advertising a plant nursery."

I whispered fiercely to Anthony. "Pull it out, boy. Quickly. This is embarrassing. Everyone is looking at us."

Anthony nodded his branches at me. "Mnn, nmng, nn," he said.

I didn't know what it meant. Probably something like, "You embarrassed *me*. Now it's your turn."

I was tempted to pull the whole thing out myself. But what if the roots grew into his tongue? I might damage his mouth.

A huge throng followed us through the shopping mall.

"Cabbage head," yelled a little kid.

"Treemendous," said someone else.

This was turning into a nightmare. I was most embarrassed. What if someone from my bowling club was watching? How humiliating.

Finally we struggled out of the shopping center and climbed onto the bus. "One and a half," I said.

The driver looked at Anthony for a long time. Then he said, "Trees are full fare."

I threw the money at him and we sat in the back of the bus. Anthony's tree head was growing all the time.

"You'll have to move," shouted the driver. "I can't see out of the back window."

Passengers were staring at us. Whispering and pointing.

I was just about to tell Anthony that this had gone far enough when I spotted something. On one of the branches. A small berry thing about the size of a marble. It was gold in color.

"An apple," I shrieked. "You're growing an apple."

I parted Anthony's branches and looked into his eyes. Then I examined the tiny fruit. "You've done it," I yelled. "You've done it. It's a Golden Gran. My new species. One of the seeds has sprouted in the cod-liver oil."

We both had tears in our eyes. Now Gran would be remembered forever, bless her heart. Anthony nodded his tree and the little apple shook about dangerously.

40

"No," I yelled. "Keep still. It's only small. It won't have any seeds yet. Don't move in case it falls off."

Anthony froze. He knew how important this was to both of us. He had loved his Gran, bless her heart. She was his favorite. "Mmn, mnng, mnff," was all he said.

"Now listen," I whispered. "The way this thing is growing, the apple should be ripe in about an hour. Then we can weed your mouth and nose. And keep the apple seeds. Then we can plant them and grow more Golden Grans. In memory of Gran, bless her heart."

"Mmnff," said Anthony. I knew that he agreed with my plan.

The bus came to a halt outside my front gate. "Walk carefully," I said. "If the apple drops off before it has grown we are finished. It might be the only one."

Anthony stood and inched along the aisle of the bus.

"Hurry up," said the driver.

"This is an emergency," I said. "We have to save the apple."

"Get moving," ordered a woman dressed in a nurse's uniform.

"We haven't got all day," said someone else.

I looked at Anthony. "Don't take any notice," I said. "Take your time."

Anthony moved forward at a snail's pace. There was no way he was going to dislodge that apple. Time passed slowly. The passengers grew restless.

In the end the driver couldn't take it any longer. He jumped out of his seat and grabbed Anthony by a lower branch. He dragged him along the bus and threw him onto the street. Then he looked at me angrily. "I'm going, I'm going," I said.

I jumped off and examined Anthony. "Are you hurt?" I yelled.

He shook his branches slowly. "Mmple," he said urgently.

"Apple," I cried. "Yes, where's the apple?" I began searching through the branches. It was still there. And it was nearly full grown.

Cameo looked on from a distance. Even the horse was interested in the apple tree.

We walked slowly into the front yard. "Five minutes more," I said. "Then we can pick the apple and weed you."

Anthony crept forward into the garden. He edged his way toward the front door. Five minutes passed. "The apple is ripe," I yelled. "Quick. Inside and I'll get some clippers."

Neither of us heard the footsteps behind until it was too late. Well not footsteps. Hoofsteps.

As quick as a flash, Cameo chomped on the apple. Swallowed it in one go. Then she tossed her head and ripped the whole tree out of Anthony's head.

"Ow!" shrieked Anthony.

Cameo trotted to the other side of the garden, still munching on the remains of the tree.

"Are you all right? Are you all right?" I called.

"Yes," Anthony screamed. "Quick, grab Cameo."

We raced across the grass but we were too late. Cameo had eaten every leaf. Every twig. Not one bit of the tree was left.

5

Well, Anthony and I just sat and stared at the floor. After all that. So near and yet so far. We had almost developed a new apple type. A Golden Gran. But Cameo had swallowed it.

"Never mind, Grandpa," said Anthony. "You'll crack it one day."

He was a great kid. He was just trying to cheer me up. But I knew it was no good. I was getting old. I didn't have much time left on earth. I knew that I would never develop the Golden Gran now. My heart was heavy.

Excuse me if I wipe a little tear from my cheek. But I always get so sad when I think of Gran, bless her heart.

Suddenly Anthony jumped up. "I know," he said. "We'll do it again. Mix up granola and cod-liver oil. And put it in our mouths. Another tree might grow."

"You'd do that for me?" I said. "Even though you hate cod-liver oil?"

Anthony nodded. "We both will," he yelled. "One of us is bound to sprout."

So that is what we did. I mixed up a new lot and we sat there with our cheeks bulging. It was lovely, was that granola and cod-liver oil mix. Or that's what *I* thought. Poor Anthony sat there with tears streaming from his eyes. He thought the taste was terrible.

For two days we sat there. Waiting and waiting and waiting. We couldn't talk. We dared not move. The phone rang but neither of us could answer it. We didn't even go outside.

Two days and two nights. Sitting there with our mouths full of granola and cod-liver oil. But nothing grew. Not a leaf. Not a twig. Nothing.

Finally Anthony got up and spat into the sink. "It's no good, Grandpa," he said. "I can't go on. It's not going to work."

He was right, of course. I spat my lot into the sink and went off and had a shower. It was the worst day of my life. I had nothing left to look forward to.

I dried myself and dressed. Then I went out into the kitchen. Just then Anthony rushed in. He was carrying something. Something wonderful.

Two golden apples. "Golden Grans," he shouted. "Look."

He pointed outside. I ran over to the window and stared out. And there it was. I couldn't believe my eyes. A magnificent apple tree growing in the backyard. Covered in Golden Grans.

The tree was sprouting out of a pile of horse manure. Cameo had done a good job.

"Whoopee," I yelled. I had never been happier in my whole life.

Anthony grinned and held out an apple. "You be the first to taste one," he said.

"No," I told him. "That honor is yours."

Anthony took a bite. He made a face and spat. "Ugh," he yelled. "Sorry, Grandpa, but it's terrible. Disgusting."

I grabbed the other apple and munched. "Delicious," I shouted. "Absolutely delicious. The first apple in the world that tastes like cod-liver oil."

WAKE UP TO YOURSELF

Look around you.

What do you see?

Maybe your bedroom with games and posters and socks on the floor?

Come on—put down the book and have a look. Right now.

Are you in the backseat of the car with your little brother next to you? Or maybe in school wishing it was time to go home? You might be outside reading under a tree. Wherever it is—have a good look.

How real is it?

What if it is a dream? Yes, really. What if you are going to wake up somewhere else and it is all gone? Mum, Dad, your pesky little brother. Teachers, school, friends. All gone and you are somewhere else.

In the real world.

What about that, eh?

They are picking teams for a football game. Oh no.

It is not one of those games run by the teachers where everyone gets a fair go. Nothing like that. No, it is a game organized at lunchtime by the kids. There are twenty-one of us lined up.

Out front are the captains—Keeble and Fitzy. They are the best football players in the school. They are big and tough and mean. If they crack a joke everyone laughs. Even when it is not funny.

Now they are picking their teams.

"Henderson," yells Fitzy. Henderson is a fantastic runner. His team will probably win. He walks out and stands next to Fitzy. He knew that he would be the first to be picked.

"Black," calls out Keeble. Robert Black is also a good football player. He is small but he is a great kicker. He grins and walks over to Keeble.

They keep calling out names.

"Swan."

"Tootle."

"Rogers."

"Tang."

Each kid walks forward when his name is called and stands next to his captain.

There are twenty-one kids. Ten per side not counting the captains. One boy will be left out. Some poor kid will not be picked. He will be left standing there and everyone will know that he is the worst football player in the school.

"Please, God, don't let it be me. Please."

There is a horrible feeling in my stomach. It feels heavy.

"Peters."

Alan Peters steps out and stands behind Keeble. What about Simon Duck? Please call Simon Duck, I think to myself. But no one calls me.

There are only a few kids in line now. We all look at each other hoping we will not be left at the end.

Now there are only two left. Me and John Hopkins.

"Hopkins," yells Fitzy. Hopkins gives a big sigh of relief and runs out in front.

Everyone looks at me standing there all alone.

"You can have plucked Duck," says Fitzy.

The kids all laugh.

"No thanks," says Keeble. "We're not that desperate."

I can feel a hot blush crawling over my face as the boys run off to start the game. I am left on my own with the little kids. Oh, the shame of it. I wish I was an ant so that I could crawl down a hole and never be seen again.

But I am not an ant so I go into the bathroom instead. I sit down in a stall where no one can see me. I stay there all lunchtime. The minutes drag by. No one knows where I am. No one cares. Finally the bell rings and I am saved. I can go to class.

2

After school I make my lonely way home. The other kids are in twos and threes but no one ever wants to walk home with me.

I think about my little brother. The one I don't have. But will soon. Mum is having a baby and I am sure it will be a boy. He will be my friend. My pal. I will look after him. Show him a thing or two. We will be the best friends in the world.

What is it about me, I wonder? Why don't I have any friends? I ask kids home but they don't come. Is it because I am no good at football? I just don't know.

I would give anything to have a friend.

I reach the front gate of our house. The grass is long and weedy. It is the worst garden in the street. I would cut the lawn for Mum but the lawn mower conked out and we can't afford to get it fixed.

To be perfectly honest, we are broke.

The phone was cut off the other day because Mum couldn't pay the bill. This is a bit of a worry.

"What if the baby comes in the middle of the night?" I say. "What then?"

Mum pats her swollen tummy. "You run down to the phone booth and ring for a taxi," she says.

"What if I'm not here?" I say.

Mum gives me a big, warm smile. "But you will be, won't you, darling?"

She is right, of course. Where else would I be? No one is going to ask me to sleep over at their place, are they? Not me. No way. To tell you the truth my heart is breaking.

We have french fries for tea. I smother mine in catsup and sit down on my mattress to watch TV. We only have one bedroom so I sleep in the living room on a mattress.

Mum is really tired. It has been a hot day and she is worn out, what with carrying the baby inside her and doing all the housework.

She is the best mum in the world. She has a great big grin when she talks. She always makes me feel that I am a sort of superhero. She wears beads and long dresses with fringe and has a little diamond stud in her nose. Sometimes she goes down the street with a flower in her hair. In bare feet too.

48

I would do anything for her. I don't mind not having a father. Mum will do. And the baby. When the baby comes I will have a pal.

But I just hope that he doesn't decide to arrive in the middle of the night.

"Go and lie down," I say to Mum. "And I will make you a nice cuppa."

Mum drinks her cup of tea and falls asleep. After a while I decide to go to bed. I jump onto my mattress and pull up the checked blanket. My eyelids begin to droop.

I start to fall asleep. Or am I falling awake? That is the question.

3

When I open my eyes I am back in the school yard and the kids are picking teams for the football game.

My mattress is on the asphalt in the school yard. I am dressed in my school clothes, not my pajamas.

"Hey, Duck," yells Fitzy. "Get up and stand in line."

I jump up, embarrassed.

Fitzy does not seem to see my mattress. No one does. Right away I know that this is a dream. Or maybe a nightmare. I am back at school and they are picking teams again.

Well, I am not going to do it. There is no way that I am going to get back in that line. And not be picked. And sit on the toilet all lunchtime. And walk home on my own all over again. This is just a bad dream and I will get out of it as quick as I can.

I decide to wake myself up. I pinch my arm. Hard. And it hurts. I do not wake up. This does not seem like a dream. It seems real. I shake my head. I pull my hair. The kids all look at me as if I am mad.

"Duck is pulling out his feathers," shouts Keeble.

A big laugh goes up. How can I get out of this? How did I get into it? On the mattress, that's how. Well, that's how I will get home.

But the mattress is fading. And so is my ticket back. I feel as if I am standing at the station and the train is going without me. Before I can move, the mattress vanishes completely. I know now that I am stuck in this dream. Or was the other world a dream? And is this the real one? I really can't tell.

All the kids are looking at me. They want to start choosing the teams. Oh no. Now I have to get in the line again. And not be picked.

But wait, what is this? There is another kid in the group who wasn't there last time. He has a cheeky grin. And on his arm is a little birthmark. It looks like a small map of Australia.

"Come on, Simon," he says with a wink. "Who wants to play football anyway?"

"Yeah," I say. "I sure don't."

"Me neither," says Tootle. He comes over with Tang, who also does not want to play.

We all grin at each other. Fitzy and Keeble are not too pleased but they don't say anything. I hope they are not going to make trouble for me after school.

I spend all lunchtime hanging out with the boy with the birthmark. It turns out that he is my best friend. His name is Matthew but I call him Possum. We have always done every-thing together—me and Possum.

After school Possum and I walk home together. We reach the front gate of a house. The grass is long and weedy. It is the worst garden in the street. It seems familiar. I feel as if I know this place. As if I should be going inside.

I open the gate.

"Where are you going?" says Possum.

I blink and scratch my head. There is an image in my head. A pretty woman with a flower in her hair. And beads. It is like a far-off dream.

I look at Possum. "To see er . . . Mum," I say.

Possum stares at me as if I have gone mad. "Simon," he says. "Your mum died when you were born."

I try to hold on to the image of a lovely lady who has a big grin whenever she talks. And a diamond stud in her nose. But the vision fades away, just like the mattress. And I am left staring at Possum with my eyes filled with tears.

"Where do I live?" I say.

Possum puts his arm around my shoulders. "Don't be a fool," he says, smiling. "You know that you live with us."

4

We walk past the house with the weedy garden and go out into the countryside. As Possum talks I remember things. How we live in a big house out of town. How his dad is a real great guy. His mum is terrific too. I call them Mum and Dad even though they aren't my real parents.

Possum and I have a room each. And our own TV. We have always been the best of pals. We are like brothers.

We take the shortcut across Crazy Mac's field when we suddenly hear something. Voices. My heart starts to pump fast and my legs feel like lead.

I know those voices. They belong to Fitzy and Keeble. Every night after school they wait for us. They are bullies. They like to scare us. "Get them," yells Fitzy.

I look at Possum. We are not fast runners. We are skinny kids. Fitzy and Keeble will catch us for sure. Then they will . . . I can't bear to think about it. I hate pain.

But Possum is not too worried. He winks at me. "The river," he whispers.

We turn and run for it. We bolt toward the river. Across the dry grass, slipping on cow pats. Stumbling, falling, scrambling up and racing on. My chest hurts because I am running so fast. I look behind and see that Fitzy and Keeble are catching up. Oh no. We are gone. Who will save us?

Possum, that's who. By the river is a huge gum tree. It has a rope hanging from a branch. The rope is hooked up on our side of the river. We can use it to swing across to the other side. Possum winks again and I know that he is the one who has put the rope there.

I do not wink back. This is no time for winking. Keeble and Fitzy are nearly up to us. There is no time for two to swing across the river. One can swing and the other will be caught.

"You go," I yell.

"No, you," says Possum.

I look down at the water. It is deep and flowing fast. I look at the safety of the other side. Fitzy and Keeble are running and shouting and waving sticks. I am scared stiff. I would love to swing away but I can't leave Possum on his own.

"Together," shouts Possum.

Fitzy throws himself toward me in a dive for my legs.

"Jump," I yell.

We grab the rope and launch ourselves over the muddy river. Fitzy crashes onto the bank with a grunt.

Down we swing, down, down, down toward the murky river. We skim across the surface and our feet trail in the water. Then up, up, up toward the opposite side. I let go and tumble onto the bank. Possum touches ground, too, but he is smart enough to hang onto the rope so that it doesn't swing back to Fitzy and Keeble.

They are angry. Furious. Crazy. Like two baboons. They jump up and down, spitting with rage on the other side of the river.

Possum makes a rude sign with his fingers. It makes Fitzy and Keeble even madder. Possum is really game. He is a great kid. He has saved us. Oh, I would do anything for Possum. He is the best pal in the world.

We walk off toward home. "What about tomorrow?" I say. "They will be waiting at the rope."

Possum walks along with a bit of a swagger. "But we won't be going that way," he says. "Will we?"

5

When we get home there is no one there. We search around for a bit and finally find the place where the chocolate-chip cookies are hidden. We take them up to my room and start munching on them.

"That river is deep," I say. "What if we had fallen in?"

"Yeah," says Possum. "We could have drowned."

"What would it be like to be dead?" I say.

Possum thinks for a bit. "I don't know," he says. "Sometimes I think that if I wasn't here no one else would be either. I can't imagine the world without me in it too."

"Yeah," I say. "Sometimes I think that it is all a dream. And that if I woke up you would be gone. Just as if you were never there."

We both stop talking and think about this for a bit. All that can be heard is the thoughtful munching of chocolate-chip cookies.

After about four cookies each we are still silent. I know that we are both thinking about the same thing. We are thinking how horrible it would be not to have each other. To be in a world without our best pal.

At that exact moment something starts to happen. Over in the corner a shape starts to shimmer and wobble. A sort of ghostly platform on the floor.

"Look at that," I yell.

"What?" says Possum.

"Something's there," I whisper. "A sort of ghost thing."

"I can't see anything," says Possum.

My mouth falls open as it takes shape. The image in the corner. It is a mattress. With a checked blanket. I know that I have seen it before.

"A mattress," I gasp.

Possum is staring at me and shaking his head.

"You sure are a funny guy, Simon," he says. "There is no mattress there."

I look at him and I look at the mattress. It seems to be calling me. But I don't want to go.

"If I get on that mattress," I say. "I will not be coming back. You will be gone. I will never see you again."

Possum is not sure whether to believe me or not. He can tell that I really think there is a mattress there. Even if he can't see it.

I feel a sort of longing. A sadness. And the picture of a

face comes into my mind. A woman with a quick smile. And beads. She is padding around in bare feet.

A voice seems to call. Like a call from way down a long drainpipe. "Simon, Simon," it says.

The picture in my mind grows stronger. The lovely lady is fat. Much fatter than normal.

"Simon," she calls in her far-off voice. "Simon, the baby is coming."

I look at Possum in panic. "The baby is coming," I say. "The baby is coming. And the phone has been cut off."

The mattress in the corner is starting to fade. Will I go or will I stay? I know that there is only one choice I can make: stay in the dream with Possum, or go back.

But then which is the dream? Maybe the other world with Mum and the baby is a dream. And this is the real one. Possum is real, I know that. Possum is my pal. He starts to scratch at the little birthmark that is like a map of Australia. His eyes grow round. He realizes that something scary is happening but he doesn't know what. "Don't go," he says. "Don't leave me, mate."

"Simon," calls the far-off voice. "Oh, Simon, quick. The baby is coming."

I can't choose. I don't know what to do. The mattress is fading fast. It will not be coming back—I know that for sure. Already the voice has sunk to a whisper. Like someone calling from a boat that is drifting out into a sea of fog.

One word fills my mind. Mum. Suddenly I run over to the mattress and jump onto it. It is warm. And real. I see Possum and the chocolate-chip cookies start to fade.

"Don't . . ." says Possum. He never finishes. Like a tear falling into the sea he drops away and is gone.

6

And I am there in the other world. The first thing I see is the plate from last night. With a few cold french fries and dried catsup. The room is small and I am on a mattress in the living room because we only have one bedroom.

Possum is gone forever. I chose this world and let his one die. A terrible sadness sweeps over me. I feel like a murderer.

But there is no time for this.

The baby is coming.

Mum collapses onto my mattress with a groan. Her nightgown is all wet. "I'll run down to the phone booth," I shout.

"Too late," says Mum. "My water has broken. It's coming."

Aw, shoot. Aw, jeez. It's coming and I am the only one here. What will I do?

I try to remember what they do on TV when babies are coming. "Push," I say. I am not sure what she is supposed to push but that is what they always seem to say.

"I am pushing," groans Mum. She is lying on her back with her knees pointing up to the ceiling.

Then I see something that I have never expected to see. Never in a million years. The top of the baby's head. It is coming out. It is covered in blood and slime and has wet hair stuck down. Oh, oh, what am I going to do?

Suddenly there is a slurping noise. More of the baby is coming out. Mum is groaning. "Push," I say.

With a sudden rush the baby is born. It is followed out by wet, bloody stuff. The baby has a long cord stuck onto its stomach. Mum has tears in her eyes. What will I do?

I lift up the baby and put it on her panting chest. Right

away it starts to cry. It is alive. It is covered in blood and gunk. But it is alive and screaming. Oh, it is terrible. Oh, it is wonderful.

"Get scissors," says Mum with a pant. "And a clothespin."

I rush off and quickly come back with the clothespin and the scissors. "Cut the cord," says Mum. I cut the cord about ten centimetres away from the baby's belly button. Then I clip it off with the clothespin.

Mum smiles. There is a terrible mess everywhere. "I'll go for help," I say.

"No," says Mum with her big grin. "In a minute. This is our special moment. Everything is all right. I have done this before, remember."

"I haven't," I say.

"Maybe not," says Mum. "But you were there the last time too. Now go and get a warm towel and we will clean the baby."

Well, everything turns out just right. I am a hero. My picture is in the paper. And on television. At school I have to give talks about how babies are born. All the kids want to be my friend. I am famous.

When they pick teams for football I am always the first one they choose. Even though I am not very good at it.

Life is wonderful. I have friends everywhere.

But now and then I feel sad. Especially when I am down by the river. I think of a pal who tied a rope to the tree so that we could escape from the bullies. A pal who loved chocolate-chip cookies.

I can see his face when he said, "Don't go." I know that I could have stayed and kept his world alive. But I didn't and my heart is heavy.

There is only one way to cheer myself up when this happens. I remember how I delivered the baby. I remember how I wiped him with the warm towel. And I remember what Mum said as she watched me cleaning him.

"Look at the little possum," she laughed. "He's got a birthmark on his arm. It looks like a tiny map of Australia."

THOUGHT FULL

"I am never eating meat again," I yelled at Dad.

He just smiled at me as if I were crazy.

You might think I'm crazy too. I mean most people who live on farms eat meat. So I'll tell you what. You be me for a while and see how you feel about it at the end.

1

It all starts because of the new steer. We have this cow called Slipped-in-the-Mud and it gives birth down in the bottom paddock. To the sweetest little calf you have ever seen.

The calf has a cute white patch on its face. It sucks away at its mother's udder and gets white froth all around its mouth.

And it likes you. It nuzzles up for a pat. Oh, it is so wonderful. It moos in a real soft way. It looks at you with those big brown eyes. Right away you decide to call it Moonbeam.

You have never loved anything like you love this little calf.

"Dad," you say. "Can Moonbeam be mine? To keep forever? Just mine? Please."

Dad shakes his head sadly. "Sorry, Bomber," he says. "We

can't afford to have it eating grass and not earning its way. Once it's weaned we have to sell it."

"There's plenty of grass around here," you yell.

"No there's not," says Dad. "We need every blade for the heifers who are going to give us milk. Steers do not grow up into cows. They become bulls. And they eat plenty."

Tears fill your eyes. You just can't stand it. "I won't let him go," you shout. But deep in your heart you know that you are only a kid. You have no power. There is nothing you can do to stop them selling Moonbeam. You run off to your room and bang the door. You are so angry that you don't come out for at least five minutes.

The next day is really the start of all the weird things that happen. You wake up in the morning to find a terrible smell in the room. In the bed in fact. You look at your hands and give a scream. Your hands are all covered in sloppy, green slime.

It stinks something terrible. How did it get there? Is someone playing a trick? What is going on here? Where did this horrible stuff come from? It looks like the goo that bubbles in the bog down by the front gate.

You think about it for a while and decide not to tell Mum and Dad about it. But it is too late. Mum is already in your bedroom and she is not overjoyed by what she sees.

"I told you to have a shower last night," says Mum angrily. "Look, your sheets are all dirty. They're covered in green slime."

"I did have a shower," you say. "Honest."

You can tell that Mum doesn't believe you. You find it hard to believe yourself. How could your hands have got so dirty when you were asleep in bed all night?

You don't worry too much about it though because you

have Moonbeam to think about. You take a walk down to his paddock for a visit. He is the best friend that you have ever had. When he licks your hand it is like being rubbed with soft, wet sandpaper. You put your arms around his neck. "I will never let them sell you," you say.

Suddenly you notice Dad standing behind you. "Don't keep going on about it, Bomber," he says. "Every animal on a farm has to earn its keep. Moonbeam has to go. Times are bad and we need every penny we can get."

Moonbeam sucks your fingers. He is only a calf. It is not his fault that he was born a male. Your heart is breaking because Moonbeam is going to be sold.

You worry about it all day and on into the evening. It is so bad that you find it hard to get to sleep that night. You toss and turn and try to hatch up plans to save your calf. In the end you nod off into dreamland.

2

At seven o'clock you are awakened by a smell. It is not the whiff of eggs and bacon sizzling in the kitchen. It is not the smell of toast. It is not the scent of a warm, summer morning. It is the stink of slimy mud. You look under the blankets. You are soaked in it. Your pajama trousers and top. Your feet and hands. A terrible, squelching green ooze. The sheets are soaked.

Your brain freezes. Someone must have sneaked into the room and dumped sloppy mud on you. But who? Mum and Dad would never do such a thing.

You grab the sheets and try to sneak down to the laundry with them before Mum sees the mess.

But you are too late.

Mum catches you. At first she doesn't say anything. She just stares at you with one of those looks that say, "How could you, Bomber?"

She calls a family conference.

This is the very worst thing. Family conferences are for times when the three of you have to work through a problem. "Communicating," says Mum.

But what it really means is that you get a big lecture.

"I slave away in that laundry," says Mum. "And Dad does the ironing. And what do you do, Bomber? You wander around outside in bare feet and make the sheets filthy. Now is that fair? I ask you."

You start to give your side of the story. "But I haven't been outside. I don't even remember—"

Dad doesn't wait for you to finish. "It's that silly calf," he says. "The boy is going down to the paddock talking to the calf in the middle of the night. It's not good enough, Bomber. As soon as that calf is weaned I'm taking it to the market."

"But—" you start to say.

"No buts," says Dad. "That calf has to go."

Nothing will change his mind. Usually Dad is reasonable. He is a great father. But nothing will make him believe that you have not been down with Moonbeam in the middle of the night.

This is ruining your life. What is going on? How are you getting dirty in your own bed? Something has to be done. And quick.

That night you go to bed as usual. Well, not quite as usual. You get your alarm clock and tie it around your neck. Then you set it for one o'clock in the morning. If someone is dumping mud in your bed you are going to be awake to catch them.

Finally you fall asleep.

3

No sooner have your eyes closed than *ding, ding, ding, ding*. What a racket. The alarm makes a terrible noise. Right away you wake up and find out that it is one o'clock.

But where are you? Everything is dark around you. Overhead there are pinpoints of light. What are they doing there on the ceiling? You look again. There is no ceiling. The lights are stars. You are outside in the cold, still night.

The wind is fresh on your cheek. The water is wet on your arms and legs.

Water?

Is this some terrible dream? No, it is not. Worst luck. Your heart sinks. You know where you are.

You are on your hands and knees scratching in the bog down by the front gate. You are covered in green gunk.

Oh no. What is going on here? Why are you outside? You must be sleepwalking. Sleepdigging. This is terrible. Horrible.

You quickly start off toward the house. But you feel uneasy. You keep looking back at the bog. It seems to be calling you. Your feet want to take you back to the disgusting, bubbling slime. It is almost as if a magnet is pulling you back. You have this terrible urge to turn around and dig in the bog.

But you are strong. You don't go. The feeling gets weaker as you move away from the bog. But it is still there all the same. Like a silent voice in your mind calling.

Just as you reach the front door you hear noise from the barn. A moo. Moonbeam.

"What the heck," you say. "I might as well go and check on him while I'm here."

You sneak into the barn and see Moonbeam curled up in the hay. Oh, he is beautiful. You start to stroke his soft, brown coat. You don't think of anything but wonderful Moonbeam. You do not realize that someone else is there too.

A hand falls on your shoulder and you just about jump out of your skin.

"Bomber. What are you doing here?"

It is Dad.

Your mind starts to race. What can you tell him? This looks bad. "I was sleepdigging," you say. "In the bog. That's where all the slime is coming from."

Dad does not believe you. That is clear. "Bomber," he says. "Don't give me that. You are sneaking out to see Moonbeam. You have used up your last chance. I am definitely taking him to the market on Saturday. This has to stop. Now get back to bed."

"But, but . . ."

It is no good. You can see by his eyes that, as usual, no buts are allowed.

You have a shower and get back into bed. You lie there thinking. Dad is going to take Moonbeam to the market. But Moonbeam is not weaned yet. How will he get milk without Slipped-in-the-Mud?

Dad doesn't want Moonbeam because he is no good for milk. Why would anyone else buy him? There is a nasty thought in the back of your mind but you can't work out what it is.

Because.

The bog is calling.

Your hands pull back the sheets. Your legs touch the floor. Your feet take you across the room. You don't want to go but you can't stop yourself. The bog. The bog. The bog.

Out into the night. Past the milking shed. Along the path to the front gate.

You find yourself staring into the slime. Frogs are croaking. Green bubbles are floating on the surface. The smell is revolting.

In your mind you scream to yourself, No, no, no.

You try to hold back. You try not to go. Your head feels as if it is filling up with water and is going to burst. The pressure is unbearable.

Suddenly you leap forward. You don't want to go but you can't stop yourself. You hit the water with an enormous splash. You fall onto your hands and knees and start digging with your fingers. You are crazy. Green water sprays everywhere. You are soaked. What are you looking for? You don't know. You don't care. Dig, dig, dig, dig. That is all you can do.

Your fingers touch something smooth. You grab it. And then it happens.

All the madness falls away. Now you are full of peace. You are happy. A wonderful feeling washes all over you. You have found it.

A bottle.

A small bottle covered in mud.

You give it a wash and tip out the bog water. The night is dark and you can't see it properly. Is this what it is all about? The sleepwalking. The digging. Just for a bottle?

Rain begins to fall so you head back to the farmhouse.

Where Dad is waiting on the front step.

He doesn't say anything. He just stands there glaring at you. He is angry. Boy, is he mad. He looks at your soaked pajamas. He thinks you have been down to see Moonbeam again.

You hold up the bottle and try to explain. "Er, sleep-digging. The bog was calling. Found this . . ."

Dad points upstairs. He only says one word.

"Bed."

5

You scamper inside as quick as you can go. You have another shower and while you are there you give the bottle a good wash.

It is just made of glass but it sure looks odd. On the bottom is strange writing. On the sides are moons and stars and bunches of grapes. The neck is swollen and shaped like the head of a witch.

You have seen a bottle like this before. It is a baby's bottle. Without the teat. But it is not a normal bottle. No way.

You fill it up with water.

Now it just needs a cap. A little teat. You sneak down to the junk cupboard and find the bottle that Mum used to feed you with when you were a baby. You take off the teat and put it on the witch bottle. Now it is complete. The teat is just like a hat on the witch's head.

You give a smile and put it under your pillow. In ten seconds you are fast asleep.

The next morning Mum and Dad do not say anything about the sleepdigging. They just stare at you without talking. They shake their heads and look at each other sadly. They are giving you the silent treatment. They are trying to make you feel guilty. And it is working.

You decide that you had better not mention the bottle. Not under the circumstances. You jump in the car and wait for Dad to drive you to school.

He is taking his time so you decide to have a little drink from the witch's hat. Just one sip. It can't do any harm. It is only water after all.

You suck away on the bottle just like a baby. The water tastes a bit strange. Bitter and sweet at the same time. Suddenly things start to happen. The countryside seems different. Colors are brighter. The wind is fresher. Bird songs are sweeter.

But not everything is an improvement. The smell from the milking shed is worse. And the bog seems to bubble and seethe with more gunk than before. The world is bigger and bolder. A little shiver runs up your spine.

Dad steps into the car and starts off. He is thinking about Moonbeam.

He is thinking about Moonbeam?

How do you know? Because you can read his mind. That's how.

You shake your head. You whack your skull with the palm of your hand. Are you going crazy or what? When you drink out of the bottle you can read people's minds.

You know every thought that Dad is thinking. He is planning to sell Moonbeam at next Saturday's sale.

"Please don't sell Moonbeam on Saturday, Dad," you say.

Dad gives you a funny look. "How did . . . ?" But he does not finish the sentence. "We have to, Bomber," he says.

"Who will buy him?" you say. "What if it's not someone nice? What if they don't love him like I do?"

Dad doesn't say anything. But a word comes into his mind. The word is *veal*.

"What's veal?" you ask.

Dad gives you another strange look. "It's meat," he answers.

"What sort of meat?" you say.

Dad doesn't say anything. He doesn't have to. You already know what is in his mind. Veal is the meat of young calves. Your heart stops inside you. Now you know why he doesn't have to wait for Moonbeam to be weaned.

"No," you scream. "No, no, no. You can't send Moonbeam off to be slaughtered."

"Look, Bomber," says Dad. "You had bacon for breakfast. Where do you think that came from?"

"That's different," you yell. "Moonbeam is almost human. He has a name. Moonbeam loves me."

Dad sighs. "Most vealers end up on the table," he says.

You feel a lump in your throat. Someone eating Moonbeam. You can't stand to think about it. "I am never eating meat again," you yell.

Dad doesn't say any more. But he keeps thinking. And you know what he is thinking because you had a drink from the bottle and can read his thoughts. He is feeling sorry for you. But he thinks that life on a farm is tough. And that you will have to get used to it. He thinks that he will take Moonbeam off to a neighbor's farm after you are asleep tonight. Then he will go to the sale yards from there.

But it won't work. Because you know what the plan is. You

68

will keep sucking from the bottle and you will know what Dad is planning to do. You will know what he is going to do before he does it. You will know his every thought. You will always be able to save Moonbeam by outsmarting Dad.

6

Dad drops you off at the school gate. Now that you have a plan you start to settle down.

So. You can read people's minds. This is going to be fun.

The first person you see is The Bot. His real name is James Blessing but everyone calls him The Bot because he borrows from people and doesn't ever pay them back.

Right away you know what he is thinking. It is amazing. You know what is going on inside his head. He has two all-day suckers in his pocket and he is going to sneak off behind the bike shed and eat one where no one can see.

"Hey, Bot," you yell. "How about one of those all-day suckers?"

He goes red in the face. A few kids gather round. "I ain't got none," he lies.

"In your pocket," you say. "In your left pocket."

A couple of kids grab him and turn out his pocket. Sure enough—two all-day suckers. The Bot goes red and hands you one.

This is great. Knowing what people think is fun. You start to lick the all-day sucker. You are very pleased with yourself.

Until you realize what The Bot is thinking. He is thinking about how his Dad is out of work. How the family doesn't have much money. How he never gets suckers like the other kids. How he was going to give the all-day sucker to his little sister.

Suddenly you feel mean. And to make it worse you know that he is thinking about how he hates being called The Bot.

He doesn't like people thinking he is stingy. He is embarrassed because his parents can't buy him things.

You wish you hadn't taken the all-day sucker. "Hey, James. You can have it back," you say.

But he just shakes his head sadly. It is too late because you have licked the all-day sucker and its colors are running.

The bell rings and everyone troops into school.

Mr. Richards is in a bad mood. You know this because you can read his mind. He is thinking about how his car had a flat tire this morning. He is thinking that anyone who did not do their homework is going to be in big trouble.

Your heart almost stops. You have not done your homework. What with all the trouble about Moonbeam you clean forgot about it.

On the other side of the room Alan Chan is checking over his answers. The homework is one of those rotten things where you read a sheet and then mark the right answers at the end.

You look at your blank sheet. You can tell what Alan Chan is thinking. He is a brain. He will get them all right. You start to mark the answers with his thoughts. Number one, A. Number two, C. And so on. It is a bit hard to get all of his thoughts because everyone else is thinking things too.

Sue Ellen is thinking about how she loves Peter Elliot.

Peter Elliot is thinking about the pimple on his nose. He is hoping that no one notices it.

Janice Roberts is also thinking about the pimple. She feels sorry for Peter Elliot because she loves him too.

Rhonda Jefferson is thinking about her dying grandma. She is very sad. She is trying to blink back the tears. You start to feel sad and have to blink back the tears too.

All of these thoughts are like static on the radio. They make it hard to tune in to Alan Chan. But in the end you check off all the answers that run through Alan Chan's brain.

7

Mr. Richards corrects the homework. He looks at the class.

"Stand up, Bomber," he says.

Your heart sinks but you stand up anyway.

"And Alan Chan," says Mr. Richards.

Alan stands up too.

"These two boys," says Mr. Richards, "got everything right. Well done, boys."

You give a big grin. Usually you have to stand up for getting nothing right. Four other kids have to stay in after school for not doing their homework.

You wonder how Alan Chan is feeling. It doesn't take long to find out. After all, you are a mind reader.

Alan is feeling tired. He is thinking about how he is not smart like everyone says. He is remembering how he stayed up all night doing his homework. He wishes that he really was a brain like everyone says.

You start to feel a bit mean.

Reading minds may not be as good as you think. And there are other problems. Everyone is thinking. Everyone.

The thoughts of all the class start to crowd in on you. Kids are thinking about sore feet, peanut-butter sandwiches, the flies on the ceiling, the swimming pool, what they had for breakfast, putting out the garbage, and how they need to go to the loo.

Most of the thoughts are boring. Some are sad. Some are things that you know you should not know. You cover your ears but that is no good. The thoughts still come pouring in. It is almost painful. You want peace from all the thoughts. It is so much of a babble that it starts to drive you crazy.

Everyone's daydreams come pouring in. Most of them are about nothing important. Shoe polish. Clouds. Drains. Suckers. Fleas. The beach. Stomachache. Hardly anyone is thinking about the lessons. Mr. Richards is wishing the bell would ring so that he can have a cup of coffee.

Thoughts, thoughts, thoughts. Noisy, nice, nasty, private, and painful. You can't stop the thoughts. The room is quiet but your brain is bursting with it all. You clap your hands over your ears but still the thoughts buzz inside your brain like a billion blowflies.

You can't stand it.

"Shut up," you yell at the top of your voice.

Everyone looks up.

"Stop thinking," you yell.

The room was already quiet. But now it is deadly silent.

The kids all think you have gone bonkers.

Mr. Richards gives you a lecture. "Thinking," he says, "is what school is all about. You could try it more often, Bomber."

You are sent out to the playground to pick up papers until you learn some manners.

At least there are no thoughts out there in the yard. Except your own.

You think about all the private things you have learned. It is like spying. It is dangerous. You find out things that you don't want to know. It is like peeping through keyholes. It is like cheating on an exam.

There is only one thing to do. The witch bottle is not to be trusted. It could cause fights. Or wars.

The bottle must never be given to another person. You are certainly not going to suck it again and neither is anyone else. Maybe you should smash it.

You hold up the bottle in your right hand. You swear a little promise to yourself. "I will never drink from this bottle again," you say. "Or I hope to die."

You are called back into class. The thoughts grow fainter and fainter. By the end of the school day you can't tell what anyone is thinking. You are glad that it has worn off. There is no way that you are going to break your oath.

Dad picks you up at the school gate.

You wonder what he is planning. It is probably about how he is going to sell your calf.

When you get home you go down and visit Moonbeam. Oh, he is lovely. Slipped-in-the-Mud gives him a lick.

You try to think of a way to save Moonbeam. Should you suck the bottle again and try to work out what Dad is up to?

No, never. And anyway, you have sworn a sacred oath.

But Dad will catch him. And sell him. To the glue factory. You think of veal. It is too horrible. If you suck the bottle you will know what Dad is up to. You can save your calf. But you can't do it. Tears come to your eyes.

You go down to the paddock to say your last good-byes. After tea Dad tries to catch Moonbeam.

He has him cornered in the barn. He approaches with a rope. He holds out the loop.

But Moonbeam slips past him and runs into the darkening

paddock. You smile to yourself. In fact you smile all evening. And the following day. Dad just can't catch Moonbeam no matter how hard he tries.

Finally, after trying all week, Dad comes rushing into the kitchen and throws his rope onto the floor. He is hot and sweaty. He is flustered. He has been chasing Moonbeam for three hours.

"We might as well keep the silly calf," says Dad. "I'll never catch it. It gets away every time. It's almost as if it can read your mind."

CLEAR AS MUD

I'm undone.

Yes, I know. I'm a fink. A rat. A creep. Nobody likes Eric Mud and it's all my own fault.

But I don't deserve this.

I look in the mirror and see a face that is not a face.

I peel back my gloves and see a hand that is not a hand.

I pull off my socks and see feet that are not feet.

I look down my pants and see . . . No, I'm not going to describe that sight.

Oh, merciful heavens. Please, please. I don't deserve this. Do I?

1

It all began with Osborn. The nerd.

See, he was a brain box. He always did his homework. He played the piano. He collected insects. The teachers liked him. You know the type.

I spotted him on his first day at school. A new kid. All alone on the end of the bench. Trying not to look worried. Pretending to be interested in what was inside his bright yellow lunch box. Making out that he wasn't worried about sitting by himself.

"Look at it," I jeered. "The poor little thing. It's got a lovely lunch box. With a Band-Aid on it. Has it hurt itself?"

The silly creep looked around the school yard. He saw everyone eating out of brown paper bags. No one in this school ever ate out of a lunch box. Especially one with the owner's name written on a Band-Aid.

Osborn went red. "G'day," he said. "I'm Nigel Osborn. I'm new here."

He even held out his hand. What a wimp. I just turned around and walked off. I would have given him a few other things to think about but my pal Simmons had seen something else interesting.

"Look," yelled Simmons. "A parka. There's a loser down on the running track wearing a parka."

We hurried off to stir up the wimp in the parka. And after that we had a bit of fun with a kid covered in pimples.

A few days went by and still Osborn had no friends. Simmons and I made sure of that. One day after school we grabbed him and made him miss his bus. Another time we pinched his glasses and flushed them down the loo.

I never missed a chance to make Osborn's life miserable. He wandered around the school yard like a bee in a garden of dead flowers. Completely alone.

Until the day he found the beetle.

2

"A credit to the whole school," said old Kempy, the school principal. "Nigel Osborn has brought honor to us, to the town. In fact to the whole nation."

I couldn't understand what he was raving about. It was only a beetle. And here was the school principal going on as if Osborn had invented ice cream.

Kempy droned on. "This is not just a beetle," he said. "This is a new beetle. A new species. It has never before been recorded." He waved the jar at the kids. What a bore.

Everyone except me peered into the bottle.

"It is an ant-eating beetle," said Kempy. "It eats live ants." He looked over at me. "Eric Mud, pay attention," he said.

I just yawned loudly and picked my teeth.

At that very moment the beetle grabbed one of the ants that was crawling on the inside wall of the jar. The beetle pushed the ant into its small mouth. It disappeared—legs twitching as it went.

Osborn stood there staring at his shoes, pretending to be modest. What a nerve. He needed to be put back in his box.

But that would have to wait. Old Kempy was still droning on. He stopped and took a deep breath. "This species will probably be named after Nigel Osborn," he said. "Necrophorus Osborn."

"Necrophorus Nerd Head," I whispered loudly. A few kids laughed.

Kempy went on with his speech. "This is the only beetle of its type ever seen. An expert from the museum is coming to fetch it tomorrow. Until then it will be locked in the science room. No one is to enter that room without permission. It would be a tragedy if this beetle were to be lost."

My mind started to tick.

A tragedy, eh?

Well, well, well.

3

It was midnight. Dark clouds killed the moon. I wrapped my fist in a towel and smashed it through the window. The sound of broken glass tinkled across the science room floor.

Once inside I flashed a beam of light along the shelves. "Where are you, beetle? Where are you, little Nerd Head?" I whispered. "Come to Daddy."

It was harder than I thought. The science room was crammed with animals in bottles. Snakes, lizards, spiders. There were so many dead creatures that it was hard to find the live one I wanted.

But then I saw it. On the top shelf. A large jar containing a beetle and some ants.

I reached up and then froze. Somewhere in the distance a key turned in a lock. The security guard. Strike. I couldn't get caught. Old Kempy had already warned me. One more bit of trouble and he would kick me out of school.

I scrambled out of the window. A jagged piece of glass cut my leg. It hurt like crazy but I didn't care. Pain never worries me. I'm not a wimp like Osborn. I ran across the running track and into the dark shadows of the night.

I held the beetle jar above my head. I had done it.

Back home in the safety of my bedroom I examined my prize. The beetle sat still. Watching. Waiting. It was covered in crazy colors—red, green, and gold—with black legs. It was about the size of a coat button.

I looked at the ants. They didn't know what was in store for them. Beetle food.

They were queer-looking ants too. I had never seen any like them before. They were sort of clear. You could see right through them. The beetle suddenly grabbed one and ate it. Right in front of my eyes.

It was funny really. This was the only one of these beetles that had ever been found. This could be the last specimen. There might be no more in the world. And in the morning I was going to flush it down the loo. What a joke.

But the next day I changed my mind. There was no hurry. I shoved the jar in the cupboard and went to school.

I played it real cool. I didn't tell anybody what I had done. You never know who you can trust these days.

Old Kempy was not too pleased. In fact he was as mad as a hornet. He gathered the whole school together in the auditorium.

"Last night," he said slowly, "someone broke into the science room and stole our beetle." His eyes roved over the heads of all the kids. He stopped when he reached me. He stared into my eyes. But I just stared back. He couldn't prove a thing. He was just an old bore.

But his next words weren't boring. Not at all. "The School Council," he said, "is offering a reward of two hundred dollars for information leading to the arrest of the thief. Or two hundred dollars for another specimen. Nigel Osborn's beetle was found in the National Park. Any beetle hunters should search there."

Old Kempy looked at Osborn. "You needn't worry, Nigel," he said. "We have photos. The new species will still be named after you."

Rats. The little wimp was still going to be famous.

I walked home slowly. An idea started to form in my head. What if I kept the beetle for a few weeks? Then I would pretend I found another one in the National Park. No one would know the difference. And I would be famous. They might even name it after me. Necrophorus Mud.

I raced home and grabbed the jar. The ants were gone. Eaten alive.

I tipped the beetle onto the table and picked it up. Its little legs waved helplessly at the ceiling. This was the beetle that was making Osborn famous. I didn't like that beetle. I gave it a squeeze.

And it bit me.

4

I yelled and dropped the beetle on the floor. I was mad. "You rotten little . . ." I said. I lifted up a boot to squash the stupid thing. Then I remembered the two hundred dollar reward. I scooped the beetle up and put it back in the jar.

I jumped into bed but couldn't sleep. My finger throbbed where the beetle had bitten me. I had a nightmare. I dreamed that I was the pane of glass in the science room window. And that someone with a towel around their fist punched a hole right through me.

I screamed and sat up in bed. It was morning.

My hand throbbed like crazy. I held it up in front of my face. I couldn't believe what I saw.

A cold wave of fear grabbed my guts. My legs trembled. My heart missed a beat.

I could see right into my finger. From the middle knuckle right down to the tip of my nail was clear. Transparent.

The bones. The tendons. The nerves and blood vessels. I could see them all. It was as if the flesh of my fingertip had changed into clear plastic.

I rubbed my eyes with my other hand. I shook my head. This was a nightmare. "Let it be a dream," I moaned. I rushed to the sink and splashed my face with cold water. Then I looked again.

It was still there.

I was a freak with a see-through finger. I felt faint. The room seemed to wobble around me.

No one in the world had a see-through finger. Kids would laugh. Sneer. Joke about me. People are like that. Pick on anyone who is different.

I couldn't tell a soul. Not my old man. Not my old lady. And especially not Simmons. I couldn't trust him an inch. He would turn on me for sure.

Breakfast was hard to eat with gloves on but I managed it. Then I headed off for school. I stumbled along the road hardly knowing where I was going. I was so upset that I didn't even feel like razzing Jug Ears Jensen. And I hardly noticed the girl with the pimples. I didn't even have the heart to give the kid in the parka a hard time.

It was just my luck to have Old Kempy for first period. "I know you're into fashion, Mud," he said. "But you might as well face it. You can't use a keyboard with gloves on. Take them off."

I can tell you my knees started to shake. I couldn't let anyone see my creepy finger. "Frostbite," I said. "I have to wear gloves."

Old Kempy gave a snort and turned away. I stuck two gloved fingers up behind his back.

5

As soon as the bell rang I bolted into the bathroom and shut myself in one of the stalls. I peeled the glove off my left hand. Perfectly normal. The flesh was pink and firm. Then, with fumbling fingers I ripped off the other glove.

I nearly fainted.

My whole hand was as clear as glass. I could see the tendons pulling. The blood flowing. The bones moving at the joints. Horrible, horrible, horrible. The beetle disease was spreading.

With shaking fingers I ripped at my shirt buttons. I couldn't bear to look. Hideous. Revolting. Disgusting.

I could see my breakfast slowly squirming inside my stomach. My lungs, like two pink bags, filled and emptied as I watched. I stared in horror at my diaphragm pumping up and down. Arteries twisted and coiled. Fluids flowed and sucked. My kidneys slowly swayed like two giant beans.

My guts revealed their terrible secrets. I could see the lot. Bare bones. Flesh. And gushing blood.

I strangled a cry. I felt sick. I rushed to the bowl and heaved. I saw my stomach bloat and shrink. The contents rushed up a transparent tube into my throat and out into the loo.

This was a nightmare.

How much of me was see-through? I inspected every inch of my body. Everything was normal down below. My legs were okay. And my left arm. So far only my stomach, chest and right arm were infected. Blood vessels ran everywhere like fine tree roots.

I wanted to check my back but I couldn't. Simmons and I had smashed the bathroom mirrors a couple of weeks ago.

The bell for the next class sounded. I was late but it didn't matter. We had Hancock for English—a new teacher just out of college. He was scared of me. He wouldn't say a thing when I walked in late.

I covered up my lungs, liver, kidneys and bones and headed off for class. So far my secret was safe. Nothing was showing.

All the kids were talking and mucking around. No one was listening to poor old Hancock. He couldn't control the class. One or two kids looked up as I walked in.

Silence spread through the room. Mouths dropped open. Eyeballs bulged. Everyone was staring at me. As if I was a freak.

Jack Mugavin jumped to his feet and let out an enormous scream. Hancock fainted. The class erupted. Running. Freaked out. Yelling. Scrambling. Scratching. They ripped at the folding doors at the back of the room. Falling over each other. Crushing. Crashing. Anything to get away from me.

What was it? What had they seen? Everything was covered. I checked myself again: hands, feet, ankles, legs, hip, chest, face.

Face?

I rushed to the window and stared at my reflection. A grinning skull stared back. A terrible throbbing specter. It was tracked with red and purple veins. My jellied nose was lined with wet bristles. A liquid tongue swallowed behind glassy cheeks. My eyeballs glared back at me. They floated inside two black hollows.

That's when I fainted.

When I awoke I remembered my dream. Thank goodness it was all over. I grinned with relief and held my hand in front of my face.

I could see straight through it.

I shouted in rage and flopped back on the bed. It wasn't a nightmare. It was real. I ripped away the crisp white sheets. I was dressed in a hospital gown. I pulled it up and examined myself. I was transparent down to the tip of my toes. I was a horrible, see-through, sideshow freak.

I rushed over to the window. A silent crowd had assembled outside. Two police cars were parked by the curb. Television cameras were pointed my way. The mob stared up at the hospital, trying to catch a glimpse of the unspeakable ghoul inside. Me.

They wanted to dissect me. Discuss me. Display me. I despised them all. Creeps. Wimps. The world was full of them.

The mob would pay hundreds for a photo. Thousands for a story. Maybe millions for an interview. They made me sick.

I knew their type.

I pulled back the curtains and stretched my bare body for all to see. Inside and out. Blood and bone. Gut and gristle. I showed them the lot.

A low moan swept through the crowd. People screamed. Cameras flashed and whirred. Clicking. Clacking. Staring. Shouting.

They leered and laughed. Mocking monsters. Ordinary people.

A doctor hurried into the room carrying a tray. He grabbed me and tried to push me back into bed. But I was too strong for him. I shoved a veined hand into his face and pushed him off. I could feel my fingers inside his mouth. He choked and gurgled as he fell. He scrambled to his feet and fled.

I pulled on my clothes and, with shirt flapping, swept down the corridor. Nurses, doctors and police grabbed at me weakly. But they had no stomach for it. Like children touching a dead animal they trembled as I passed.

The crowd at the curb fell back in horror. I raised my arms to the heavens and roared. They turned and ran, dropping cameras and shopping bags. Littering the road with their fear.

I set off down the empty streets. Loping for home. Looking for a lair.

It wasn't far to go. I kicked the front door open and saw my old lady standing there. She tried to scream but nothing came out. She turned and ran for her life. She hadn't even recognized her own son.

I growled to myself. I pushed food into a knapsack. Meat. Bread. Clothes. Boots. A knife.

And the beetle—still in its jar.

I charged out into the backyard and scrambled over the fence.

Then I headed for the mountains.

7

Up I went. Up, up, up into the forest. No one followed. Not at first.

The sun baked the road to powder. The bush waited. Buzzing. Shimmering. Slumbering in the summer heat.

I was heading for the farthest hills. The deepest bush. A place where no one could see my shame. I decided to live in the forest forever.

No one was going to gawk at me. I hated people who were different. And now I was one of a kind.

When my food ran out I would hunt. There was plenty to eat. Wallabies, possums, snakes. Even lyrebirds.

After five or six hours of trudging through the forest I started to get a strange feeling. Almost as if I was being followed.

Every now and then a stick would break. Once I thought I heard a sort of a howl.

I crawled underneath a fern and waited.

Soon the noises grew louder. I *was* being followed. I grabbed my knife and hunched down ready to spring.

Scatter. Jump. Lollop. Dribble. Would you believe it was a dog? A rotten half-grown puppy scampered into view.

"Buzz off," I yelled. "Scram. Beat it." The stupid dog jumped around my feet. I kicked at it but missed. It thought I was playing.

The last thing I wanted was a dog. Yapping and giving me away. I threw a stone at it and missed. The dog yelped off into the bush.

But it didn't give up. It just followed a long way back. In the end I gave up. I could teach it to hunt and kill. It might be useful.

"Come here, Hopeless," I said.

The stupid thing came and licked my arm. Its tongue flowed along my clear liquid skin. It didn't seem to mind that I was transparent. Dogs don't care if their owners are ugly. Inside or out.

The night fell but I dared not light a fire. I huddled in a blanket inside a hollow tree. Hopeless tried to get in to warm himself but I kicked him out. The mutt probably had fleas.

I found a couple of ants in the wood.

Food.

But not for me. I opened the jar and dropped the ants inside. Then I watched the beetle stuff its dinner into its mouth.

I looked at the beetle with hatred. It had caused all this trouble. I was going to make it pay. "One day," I said. "One day, little beetle, I am going to eat you."

For three weeks I tramped through the forest. Deeper and deeper. There were no tracks. No signs of human life. Just me and Hopeless. We ate possums and rats and berries. At night we shivered in caves and under logs.

There were leeches, march flies. Cold. Heat. Dust. Mud. On and on I went. The ugly boy and the stupid dog.

Sometimes I would hear a helicopter. Dogs barking. A faint whistle on the air. But in the end we left them far behind. We were safe. Deep in the deepest forest.

I found a cave. Warm, dry, and empty. It looked down onto a clear rushing river. There would be fish for sure.

Hopeless liked the cave too. The stupid mutt ran around sniffing and wagging its tail.

It was the first laugh I'd had for ages. Oh, how I laughed. I cackled till the tears ran down my face. To see that dog wag its tail. Its long, clear tail. With the bones showing through the skin. And veins weaving their way in and out.

Hopeless had the see-through disease. What a joke. It was catching.

In the morning most of the dog was see-through. The only bit to stay normal was its head. It had a hairy dog's head but the rest of it was bones, and lungs and kidneys and blood vessels. Just like me. I held up a bit of dead possum. "Beg," I said. "Beg."

It did too. It sat up and begged. But I didn't give it the possum. There wasn't enough to share around.

8

We stayed in that cave for ten years. The three of us. Me, Hopeless, and the beetle. I was like Robinson Crusoe. I set up the cave with homemade furniture. In the end it was quite comfortable.

Every day I fed that beetle. Two ants a day. I kept him alive for ten years—can you believe it? And every day I told the beetle the same thing. "When I am twenty-four," I told it, "I am going to eat you. To celebrate ten years in the bush."

Not once did I think of going back to civilization. I wasn't going to be a joke. Looked at. Inspected.

And once they found out that the disease was catching, no one would come near me anyway. They would lock me up. Put me in quarantine. Examine me like a specimen. I could never go back.

I was fourteen when I went into that forest.

And I was twenty-four when I left it.

See, it happened like this. On my twenty-fourth birthday I decided to have a little party. A special meal just for me. Something I had been looking forward to for many years.

I grabbed the beetle jar and made a speech. "Beetle," I said, "I am an outcast. An ugly, see-through monster. I have lived here with you and Hopeless for ten years. In all that time I have not seen a human face. I haven't heard a spoken word. I want to go home but I can't. Now I pass sentence on you. I sentence you to be eaten alive. Come to Daddy, beetle."

The beetle waved its legs. It almost seemed to know what

me back into a creepy horror? He had just licked my face. I might catch the disease back from Hopeless.

I sat down and thought about it. There was no way I was going to go home unless I was completely cured. I decided to stay for another month. Just to be on the safe side.

Every night I slept with Hopeless. I breathed his breath. I even shared his fleas. But nothing happened. I stayed normal. And Hopeless stayed see-through.

You couldn't get the disease twice. It was like measles or mumps. You couldn't catch it again.

Maybe if the beetle bit you again you would get it. But the beetle was dead. There was no way I would ever be a freak again.

I packed up my things and headed for home.

9

This was going to be great. I would be famous. The return of the see-through man. And his dog.

I would be normal. But not Hopeless. He was still a walking bunch of bones and innards. I could put him on show. Charge hundreds of dollars for a look. People would come from everywhere to see the dog with the see-through stomach. I would be a millionaire in no time. Hopeless was a valuable dog.

It was a tough trip back through the deep undergrowth and rugged mountains.

But finally the day came.

Hopeless and I stood on the edge of a clearing and stared at a building.

It was a little rural school—the type with one teacher and

was going to happen. I tipped it out of the jar and put it insi
my mouth. I held up my mirror and watched it roaming abc
in there. I could see it through my clear, clear cheeks.
sniffed and snuffed. It searched around trying to find a w
out. It had a look down the hole at the back but didn't l
what it saw. It backed out.

Then it bit me on the tongue.

I screamed and spat the beetle out onto the floor of
cave. I stamped on it with my boot and squashed it into pɪ
Then I rinsed my mouth out with water from the creeł
spat and coughed.

The pain was terrible. My tongue started to swell. I ł
the mirror up to my face. I stuck out my tongue to get a gɪ
look because I couldn't see it properly through my cheeł

I couldn't see it properly through my cheeks?

I couldn't see it at *all* through my cheeks.

A pinkish blush was spreading over my face. Eyelids. I
A nose. My skin was returning to normal. I couldn't see
spine. My skull was covered by normal hair and flesh. My
sprouted a dark beard.

I just sat there and watched as the normal color sl
spread over my body. Skin, lovely skin. It moved dowr
neck. Over my chest. Down my legs.

By the next day I was a regular human being. Not a kiɪ
or lung to be seen. One bite of the beetle had made me
through. And another had cured me.

I could go home. I looked like everyone else again.

Hopeless came and licked me on the face. I pushed
away with a scream.

The dog was still clear. I could see a bit of bush rat pa
through his stomach.

He was still see-through. What if he reinfected me? Tu

about fifteen kids. It was a perfect place for me to reappear. They would have a phone. They could notify the papers. And the TV.

The man from the mountains could go home in style.

Still, I was worried. I mustn't frighten them. Hopeless was a scary sight. The teacher and kids would never have seen a dog with its guts showing before. I decided to tie Hopeless up. I didn't want anything to happen to him.

But I was too late. Hopeless bounded off across the grass toward the school.

"Come back, you dumb dog," I yelled. "Come back or I'll put the boot into you."

Hopeless didn't take a bit of notice. He charged across the grass and into the school building.

I waited for the screams of horror. Waited for the students to flee out of the building and run down the road. Waited for the yelling and the fainting.

What if the teacher shot Hopeless? I wouldn't have anything to show. A dead dog was no good.

"Don't," I yelled. "Don't." I ran and ran.

Then I stopped outside the window. I heard excited voices.

"Good dog. Good dog," said a child's voice.

"Here, boy," said another.

Something was wrong. They weren't scared of him. Surely Hopeless hadn't changed back too. It couldn't happen that quickly.

I charged into the schoolroom.

The teacher and the kids were all patting Hopeless. His guts still swung about in full view. His dinner still swirled in his stomach. The bones in his tail still swished for all to see.

But the kids weren't scared.

Not until they saw me.

A little girl pointed at me and tried to say something. Then they began screaming. Shouting. Clawing at the windows. They were filled with horror. They had never seen anything as horrible as me before.

The teacher could see that the kids were terrified.

"Out the back," he yelled at the children. "Quickly."

The kids charged out of the back door and the teacher followed.

I was alone in the schoolroom.

I looked at the pictures of the see-through people on the walls. I looked at the photographs of the see-through people in the textbooks. In India. In China. And England.

I looked at the photograph of our see-through prime minister. And America's see-through president.

I stared out of the window at the see-through children running in fear down the road. Followed by a perfectly normal see-through dog.

And I realized then. As I realize now. That I am the only person in the world who has their innards covered by horrible pink skin.

I am still a freak.

And I don't deserve it.

Do I?

WHAT A WOMAN

1

For some reason it gave Sally the creeps.

It was made of brass and was about the size of a matchbox. It was heavy and had the initials S.O. carved in the top. Her dad used it to hold down his papers. Sally shivered and put the little paperweight back on the desk.

"I told you not to play with that, Sally," said Dad. "It's the only thing I have to remind me of Aunt Esso."

Sally sighed and looked out of the window at the sheep grazing along the side of the road. "Here's the school bus," she said. She grabbed her bag and slowly walked out of the door.

She didn't want to go to school. She never wanted to go to school. She hated it. She knew she had to go. She wanted to be a doctor and there aren't too many doctors who haven't been to school. But at times she felt like skipping it.

There were only sixteen students in the school: four boys in the youngest grades, three boys in grade four, two boys in grade five, and six boys in grade six. That made fifteen boys.

Fifteen boys and one girl. All in the same little classroom with one teacher. And he was a man.

And today they were practicing for the Mini-Olympics. Shot put, long jump, high jump, one hundred meters, and marathon. Sally would come in last as usual. The six boys in grade six would all beat her in every event. Even some of the little kids would sometimes come in ahead of her.

And Jarrod Olsen would sneer and snigger and show off when Mr. Rickets wasn't looking. "What a woman," he would say as Sally finally crossed the finish line.

And that's the way it turned out. Sally was very small for her age. She just didn't seem to have the strength to keep up. She tried especially hard in the shot put. But in the end she came in last in every event—trailing in behind the boys.

"Don't worry about it," said Mr. Rickets with a smile. "You are better at other things. It's just bad luck that there are no other girls for you to compete against."

"Bad luck," said Sally. "It sure is."

On the way home in the bus it was the same as usual.

"Last in the shot put," yelled Jarrod Olsen.

"Last in the long jump," hooted Graeme Arndt.

"Last in the high jump," smirked Daniel Basset.

"Last in the hundred meters," shouted Harry Vitiolli.

"Last in the marathon," said Richard Flute.

Then the boys all took a deep breath and shouted out together, "What a woman!"

It made Sally so mad. The way they said the word *woman* as if there was something wrong with it. Sally could feel tears pricking at the back of her eyes. She had to hold them back. She couldn't let the boys see her cry. They would never let her forget it.

But a single tear, one rotten little tear, gave her away. It rolled down her cheek and plopped onto her schoolbag.

Jarrod Olsen jumped forward and put the end of his finger in the tear. He held it up for all to see. "Look at that," he shouted. "What a woman. Weak as water."

The boys rolled around laughing. How Sally hated those bus trips. They seemed to go on forever. Past the empty fields and along the never-ending road.

But at last the bus stopped at her farm gate and Sally jumped down. She just couldn't think of anything to say. Nothing seemed to shut those boys up. They thought they were tough.

If only she could win one event in the Mini-Olympics. Just one. Then she could hold her head high.

But she knew she never would.

"It's only attitude," said Dad. "You'll never win if you think you'll lose. You have to be positive."

"I am positive," said Sally. "I'm positive that I'm no good at sports."

She picked up the little brass paperweight. "Can I borrow this?" she asked. "I have to give a talk at school. It can be about anyone in our family. I'm going to talk about Aunt Esso."

"No way," said Dad. "You might lose it."

"Go on," said Mum. "Let her. It's an interesting story. And I'd like to see her get a better mark than those horrible boys."

In the end her dad gave in. "But don't let it out of your sight," he said. "Or you're history, Sally."

Sally looked at the class. She held up the little brass paper-weight in the palm of her hand. "This belonged to my Aunt Esso," she said. "She was good at sports. Really tough, too."

"I'll bet," whispered Jarrod Olsen.

Sally went red but she kept going. "She won trophies for everything. Horseback riding. Football. Cricket. Woodchopping. You name it—and she was the champion."

"A woman couldn't win woodchopping," said Jarrod Olsen in a loud voice.

"Jarrod," said Mr. Rickets. "Don't interrupt."

"She had a lucky charm," said Sally. "A tiny horseshoe brooch which brought her luck. She wore the brooch to every event. And she always won. Except once."

Sally stopped. She hadn't meant to say that bit.

"What happened, Sally?" asked Mr. Rickets.

"She lost her lucky brooch. When she went into the wood-chopping that year she didn't have it with her. She lost her brooch. And her luck. The ax missed and she cut off her toe. After that she couldn't go in anything. Not without her lucky charm."

A great roar of laughter went up. All the boys fell about laughing. Except Jarrod Olsen. He went pale in the face. His skin turned sweaty. He looked as if he was going to faint. His mouth opened and closed like a goldfish.

"Are you all right, Jarrod?" said Mr. Rickets. He led Jarrod to the nurse's office and gave him a drink of water.

"Just felt a bit hot," said Jarrod Olsen when he came back. He was as cocky as ever.

"I thought you were going to faint," said Mr. Rickets.

"No way," said Jarrod. "Only girls faint."

That afternoon it was more Mini-Olympics. All the kids lined up. Youngest to oldest. Sally shoved her Aunt Esso's paperweight into the pocket of her tracksuit. It made the pocket bulge but there was no way she was going to part with it.

What if someone stole it? Dad would never forgive her. Aunt Esso had died a year after the accident with the ax. The little paperweight was all Dad had to remind him of her. No one had ever found the lost lucky charm.

First, the kids all took their turn at throwing the heavy shot put. The little kids could only throw it a meter or so.

Jarrod Olsen was the best by far. He made four-and-a-half meters.

Usually Sally didn't like waiting for her turn. She hated them all watching when she only threw the shot put the same distance as the little kids. But today she felt lucky.

She grabbed the shot put and tucked her hand into her shoulder. She bent back and then heaved. The shot put seemed light. Not nearly as heavy as usual. It soared through the air and thumped into the grass.

"Five meters," yelled Mr. Rickets. "Sally is the winner."

The boys went silent. Not one person said, "What a woman."

Jarrod Olsen just whispered, "Fluke."

Next it was the long jump. Sally patted her pocket while she waited her turn. She felt lucky again. At last it was her turn. She started to run. Oh, how she ran. Her legs felt light. They bore her along the track at terrific speed. Up she went. Soaring through the air and landing in the sand far beyond any of the boys' marks.

"Sally wins again," said Mr. Rickets. "Good work, Sally."

Sally smiled and felt the paperweight in her pocket. "What

have you got there, Sally?" said Mr. Rickets. "You shouldn't run with a sharp object in your pocket."

"It's Aunt Esso's paperweight," said Sally.

Mr. Rickets took it from her hand and examined it carefully. "It's not a weight, Sally," he said. "It's a box. A trick box. I've seen one of these before. You have to try and open the lid. There's a knack to it. If you press in the right spot the lid will spring open."

He handed it back. "There could even be something inside," he said.

Sally pressed the box and twisted it all afternoon. But there was no way she could open the lid. If there was a trick it was certainly a good one.

That night Sally told her mum and dad what Mr. Rickets had said. Dad shook the box and held it up to his ear. "He's right, by golly," said Dad. "I think there is something inside. I wonder what it is."

Just then the phone rang. It was Mr. Ralph, the president of the football club. Dad smiled as he talked into the phone. "For you," he said to Sally. "This is your lucky day."

Sally listened with a widening grin. "Thanks, Mr. Ralph," she said. She put down the phone and started to yell. "Whoopee. I've won a bike in the football raffle."

She grabbed Aunt Esso's brass box. "Can I hang on to this for a while?" she said. "Until I find out how to open it. I'm dying to know if there's anything inside."

4

The next day was great for Sally.

Dad took her to school so she didn't have to listen to Jarrod Olsen and the boys taunting her on the bus.

She stepped out of the truck and saw something blowing along the road. "Ten dollars," she yelled. "Fantastic."

As she walked into the school the wind blew a tile off the roof. It whizzed past her head and hit Peter Monk on the knee. Blood poured down his leg. He dropped to the ground, yelling and screaming.

Sally, who loved dressing wounds, whipped out her handkerchief and stopped the flow of blood.

When all the fuss was over Mr. Rickets gave Sally a warm smile. "Sally did a great job," he said. "A lot of people would have fainted at the sight of that wound."

"Only girls would faint," whispered Jarrod Olsen in a mean voice.

"You were lucky, Sally," said Mr. Rickets. "If that tile had hit you on the head you could have been killed."

Sally grinned and took out Aunt Esso's box. She twisted and pushed. She rattled it and held it up to her ear. She tried everything she could think of but nothing would make the top spring up.

But it didn't matter. This was her lucky day.

And there was one thing she was looking forward to. The marathon.

If she could beat just one or two of the boys it would be great. And if she could beat Jarrod Olsen it would be even better. He thought he was so tough. So smart. So superior. Just because he was big. Just because he had bulging muscles. Just because he was a boy.

If she won the marathon she could prove once and for all that girls were not weaker than boys. She prodded once again at Aunt Esso's brass box. But nothing happened. She was just bursting to know if anything was inside.

"Okay," said Mr. Rickets. "Everyone get changed for the marathon."

5

Sally went alone into the girls' changing room. There was no one to talk to. No one to share her problems with. No one to trust with her hopes. She shoved the brass box into her track-suit pocket and tried not to listen to the loud talk coming from the other side of the wall.

Jarrod Olsen's voice was the loudest, as usual. "I bet Sally-What-a-Woman comes last again," he said.

Sally could hear the others laughing. How embarrassing. She went over to the sink and splashed water on her face.

Then she froze.

In the sink she saw something twinkle. Down the plug hole. In the gloomy water there was a flash. She bent down and twisted the plug on the S-bend. Filthy water gushed out.

And so did a filthy diamond ring. It was covered in slime but Sally could see at once that it was made of gold. What luck.

"If no one claims it, it's yours," said Mr. Rickets. "Worth a bundle, I should think. Today's your lucky day. Okay, now line up with the boys for the start of the marathon."

"What a woman," whispered Jarrod Olsen. His friends all laughed behind their hands.

Sally patted her pocket. She felt lucky. The marathon was

only for the older kids. It was a long way to run. It took stamina. She was going to show these boys what toughness really was.

"Go," yelled Mr. Rickets.

Jarrod Olsen shot straight to the front. He always won these events. But not today. Sally was just behind him.

She felt wonderful. Like a winner. Lucky. Usually her heart banged painfully in her chest but today she felt only happiness.

She jogged along behind Jarrod Olsen, happy to stay in second place. For now.

The other boys all fell behind. Soon there were just the two of them jogging along the dusty country road.

Jarrod turned and saw Sally on his heels. Sweat was running down his face. He was puffing and seemed tired. But he still managed to grunt out his usual insults. "Playing with the boys, are we, Sally-What-a-Woman?" he sneered. "There's a long way to go yet."

Sally could feel Aunt Esso's box in her pocket. Oh, she was going to enjoy this race. Enjoy showing these boys how tough a girl could be. If only she could win.

They turned off into the bushland along a track. Jarrod Olsen still led the way. Sally decided to make a break for it. She turned on the power. Her best effort. She drew alongside Jarrod Olsen. Their feet thumped in unison. Jarrod suddenly swerved over, forcing Sally into shrubs.

She stumbled but kept her feet. Once again she drew level, now ready to pass.

Sally strained. Her hair was plastered to her face. Her breath tore at her chest. Her side hurt. Her legs ached. Side by side they ran. She just couldn't seem to find that extra bit of speed.

Sally reached into her pocket and grasped Aunt Esso's box in her hand. She felt a small surge of power and started to move ahead.

Suddenly Jarrod Olsen made his move. He kicked out with one foot. And Sally fell. The box tumbled from her hand and bounced along the track. A searing pain shot up from her ankle into her leg.

Jarrod stopped and picked up the shining box.

"Give that back," Sally yelled through the pain. She could feel a tear trying to escape and desperately tried to hold it back.

The boy just stood there gloating with his eyes. Then he shoved the box into his pocket. "I knew you couldn't stand the pace," he said. "What a woman."

He turned and trotted away.

"My box," shrieked Sally. "Give it back."

But the only answer was a laugh that followed Jarrod around a tree and out of sight.

6

Sally managed to stand. But the pain in her ankle was terrible. She started to hobble on. All the boys passed her. Every one.

By the time she got back they were all waiting at the finish line. Drinking from cans and fooling around. "Sally-What-a-Woman is last again," yelled Jarrod.

"Weak."

"Pathetic."

The insults came thick and fast until Mr. Rickets put a stop to it. "Sally has done well for a girl," he said.

Sally winced at his words. Oh, how she wanted to show those males. They thought they were so tough. All of them. She felt a blind fury rising up inside her. A black cloud of anger misted her eyes.

"He stole my box," she yelled.

"I only carried it back for her," lied Jarrod. "After she pretended to fall over. She is so weak."

More than anything in the world Sally wanted to show those boys that she wasn't weak. Just once. But her luck seemed to have run out. If only she could get her box back.

Jarrod started to fiddle around with the letters on top of the box. Suddenly the letter *S* moved.

And a little lid sprang up.

Everyone crowded over to look. Jarrod peered inside. "There's something ins . . ." he started to say.

He never finished his sentence. He went pale in the face. His skin turned sweaty. He looked as if he was going to faint. His mouth opened and closed like a goldfish. And then he did faint. Out like a light.

All the boys crowded around the box where it had dropped onto the grass. One by one they turned pale. And collapsed.

Mr. Rickets ran over. He grabbed the box, turned gray, and staggered a few steps. Then he fainted too.

Sally ran over and picked up the box. She peered inside. She stared at the males—all unconscious on the grass. Every one of them had fainted. Mr. Rickets lay there with his eyes rolled back. They all looked so ridiculous.

Suddenly Sally didn't care about the race. Or coming first. Or being the only girl in the school.

She smiled to herself. Never again would anyone at this school say to her, "What a woman" in quite the same way.

And in that moment she knew that toughness had nothing to do with muscles. And winning had nothing to do with luck.

She put one foot on Jarrod Olsen's chest. "What a bunch of weakies," she said to herself. "Anyone would think they had never seen a toe before."

YOU BE THE JUDGE

A person who eats someone else is called a cannibal. But what are you called if you drink someone? Like I did.

No, no, no. Don't put down the book. This isn't a horror story. It isn't even a horrible story. And it's not about vampires and ghouls. But it sure is a weird tale. Really weird.

Now you can say that you don't believe me if you like. But I tell you this—I don't tell lies. Well, that's not quite true. I did tell one once. A real big one. Did I do the right thing? I don't know. You be the judge.

1

It began the day Dad and I moved to the end of the world.

There we were. In the middle of the desert. The proud new owners of the Blue Singlet Motel. There was no school. There was no post office. There was no pub. There were no other kids. There was nothing except us and our little cafe with its gas pumps. And two rooms out the back for rent.

The red desert stretched off in every direction.

And it was hot. Boy was it hot. The heat shimmered up off

the sand. When you walked outside you could feel the soles of your shoes cooking.

"Paradise," said Dad. "Don't you reckon?"

"Ten million flies can't be wrong," I said, waving a couple of hundred of them away from my face.

"Don't be so gloomy," said Dad. "You'll love it. The trucks all stop here on their way to Perth. It's a little gold mine."

Just then I noticed the dust stirring in the distance. "Our first customer," said Dad. A huge truck was buzzing toward us at great speed. Dad picked up the nozzle of the gas pump. "He'll probably want about a hundred liters," he said with a grin.

The truck roared down the road. And kept roaring. Straight past. It vanished into the lonely desert.

Poor old Dad's face fell. He put the nozzle back on the pump. "Don't worry," he said. "There'll be plenty of others."

But he was wrong. For some reason hardly any of the trucks pulled up. They just tore on by. There were a few tourists. They stopped and bought maps and filled up their water bottles and got gas. Some even stayed the night. It was a living. But it wasn't a gold mine.

But to be honest it wasn't too bad. And Dad had a plan. A plan to attract customers.

2

"It's called a Wobby Gurgle," Dad said, waving an old, faded book at me. "There's a legend that the Wobby Gurgle lives around here in the desert."

"What's it look like?" I said.

Dad looked a bit embarrassed. "No one's ever seen one," he said.

"Well, how do you know there's any such thing?"

"Stories," said Dad. "There are stories."

"Well, what does a Wobby Gurgle do?" I asked.

"Drink."

"Drink?"

"Yes," he went on. "It, ah, likes to drink water."

I scoffed. "There isn't any water around here. Only what we bring in by truck. There isn't a water hole for hundreds of miles."

Dad wasn't going to give up. "Well, maybe it sort of saves water up. Like a camel."

"It would have to be big. It hasn't rained here for twelve years," I told him.

Dad tried to shush me up. He was getting all excited. "Imagine if it was true," he said. "People would come from everywhere to see it. We could sell films and souvenirs. Lots of gas. We could open a museum. Or a pub."

Dad was getting excited. His face was one big happy grin.

"Like the Loch Ness Monster," he yelped. "No one's ever really seen it. But people go to Loch Ness from all over the world—just hoping to catch a glimpse."

"So?" I said.

"So we let people know about the Wobby Gurgle. They'll come for miles to see it."

"But what if there isn't one?" I said. "Then you would be telling a lie."

Dad's face fell. "I know," he said. "But we'll keep our eyes open. If we see one it will be like hitting the jackpot."

3

Well, we didn't see anything. Not for a long time anyway. Time passed and I started to enjoy living at the Blue Singlet Motel. We didn't make a lot of money. But we got by.

I liked the evenings the best. After the sun went down and the desert started to cool. Sometimes a gentle breeze would blow in the window. I would sit there staring into the silent desert, wondering if anything was out there.

"Never go anywhere without a water bottle," Dad used to say. "You never know what can happen out here in the desert."

Anyway, this is about the time that things started to get weird. One night I filled my water bottle to the brim and put it on the windowsill as usual. I fell off to sleep quickly. But something was wrong. I had bad dreams. About waterfalls. And tidal waves. And flooding rivers.

I was drowning in a huge river. I gave a scream and woke up with a start. I was thirsty. My throat was parched and dry. I went over to my water bottle and opened it.

Half the water was gone.

I examined it for holes. None.

Who would do such a thing? Dad was the only other person around and I could hear him snoring away in his bedroom. He would never swipe my water. He was the one always giving me a lecture about never leaving the property without it.

I looked at the ground outside. My heart stopped. There on the still-warm sand was a wet footprint.

I opened my mouth to call out for Dad. But something made me stop. I just had the feeling that I should handle this myself. It was a strange sensation. I was scared but I didn't tell Dad.

I jumped out of the window and bent over the footprint. I touched it gently with one finger.

Pow. A little zap ran up my arm. It didn't hurt but it gave me a fright. It was like the feeling you get when lemonade bubbles fizz up your nose. Like that but all over.

I jumped back and looked around nervously. The night was dark. The moon had not yet risen. All around me the endless desert spread itself to the edges of the world.

The warm sand seemed to call me. I took a few steps and discovered another footprint. And another. A line of wet footprints led off into the blackness.

I wanted to go home. Turn and run back to safety. But I followed the trail, still clutching the half-empty water bottle in my hand.

4

How could someone have wet feet in the desert? There was no pond. No spring. No creek. Just the endless red sand.

The footprints followed the easiest way to walk. They avoided rocks and sharp grasses. On they went. And on.

I was frightened. My legs were shaking. But I had to know who or what had made these prints. I was sure that a Wobby Gurgle had gone this way.

I could run and get Dad, but the trail would have vanished by then. The tracks behind me were evaporating. In a few minutes there would be no trail to follow.

If I could find a Wobby Gurgle we would be set. Visitors would come by the thousands.

A cricket chirped as I hurried on. A night mouse scampered

out of my way. Soon the cafe was only a dark shadow in the distance. Should I go on? Or should I go back?

I knew the answer.

I had to go back. It was the sensible thing to do. Otherwise I might be gobbled up by the desert. I was in my pajamas and slippers—and only had half a bottle of water. That wouldn't last long. Not once the sun came up.

The footprints were fading fast. I looked back at the cafe. Then I headed off in the opposite direction, following the tracks into the wilderness.

I had never been one to do the sensible thing. And anyway, if I could spot a Wobby Gurgle we would make a fortune. Tourists would come from everywhere to look for it. That's what kept me going.

On I went and on. The moon rose high in the sky and turned the sand to silver. The Blue Singlet Motel vanished behind me. I was alone with the wet footprints. And an unknown creature of the night.

The moon started to lower itself into the inky distance. Soon the sun would bleach the black sky. And dry the footprints as quickly as they were made. I had to hurry.

My eyes scoured the distance. Was that a silvery figure ahead? Or just the moon playing tricks?

It was a tree. A gnarled old tree, barely clinging to life on the arid plains. I was disappointed but also a little relieved. I wasn't really sure that I wanted to find anything.

I decided to climb the tree. I would be able to see far ahead. If there was nothing there I would turn around and go home. I grabbed the lowest branch of the tree.

5

I can't quite remember who saw what first.

The creature or me.

I couldn't make any sense of it. My mind wouldn't take it in. At first I thought it was a man made of jelly. It seemed to walk with wobbly steps. It was silvery and had no clothes on.

It let out a scream. No, not a scream. A gurgle. Well, not a gurgle either. I guess you could call it a scurgle. A terrifying glugging noise. Like someone had pulled out a bath plug in its throat.

It was me that let out a scream. Boy, did I yell. Then I turned and raced off into the night. I didn't know where I was running. What I was doing. I stumbled and jumped and ran. I felt as if any moment a silvery hand was going to reach out and drag me back. Eat me up.

But it didn't. Finally I fell to the ground, panting. I couldn't have moved another step, even if I'd wanted to. I looked fearfully behind me. But there was nothing. Only the first rays of the new day in the morning sky.

Soon it would be hot. Unbearably hot. I stood up and staggered on toward where I thought the Blue Singlet Motel should be.

I wandered on and on. The sun rose in the sky and glared down on me. As I went a change came over me. My fear of the Wobby Gurgle started to fade. And be replaced by another terror. Death in the desert. I was hopelessly lost.

The water bottle was warm in my hand. I raised it to my lips and took a sip. I had to make it last.

By now my face was burning. Flies buzzed in my eyes. My mouth felt as if I had eaten sand for breakfast. My slippered feet were like coals of fire. My breath was as dry as a dragon's dinner.

Stupid, stupid, stupid. To leave home in the middle of the night. With only a little water. And no hat. Dressed in pajamas. The heat was making me crazy.

How long I walked for I couldn't say. Maybe hours. Maybe days. My throat screamed for water. In the end I guzzled the lot in one go. I was going mad with thirst.

I laughed crazily. "Wobby Gurgle," I shouted. "Come and get me. See if I care."

Finally I stumbled upon a small burrow under a rock. There was just enough room for me to curl up in its shade. I knew that without help I would never leave that spot.

6

Night fell. I dozed. And dreamed. And swallowed with a tongue that was cracked and dry. I dreamed of water. Sweet water. I was in a cool, cool place. A wet hand was stroking my face. A lovely damp hand, fresh from a mountain stream.

I opened my eyes.

It wasn't a dream.

Or a nightmare.

It was the Wobby Gurgle.

Normally I would have screamed and run. But in my near-dead state I only smiled. Smiled as if it was perfectly normal to see a man made of water.

He had no bones. No blood. No muscles. His skin was like clear plastic. The nearest image I can think of is a balloon filled with water. But a balloon shaped like a man. With arms and legs and fingers. All made of water.

For a silly second I wondered what would happen if I stuck a pin in him. Would he collapse in a shower and seep away into the sand?

His water lips smiled sadly. His hand on my cheek tingled like fizzing snow. Cool, cool, so cool.

Inside his chest a tiny, dark red fish circled lazily. I knew that I must be losing my mind. There is no such thing as a man made of water. With a fish swimming inside him.

It was then that he did the weirdest thing of all. He placed the end of one finger into my mouth. It was cold and fresh and filled me with sparkling freshness. A little electric shock ran all over me.

I felt a trickle of pure water on my tongue. The clearest, coolest, freshest water in the world. I sucked like a calf at a teat. The Wobby Gurgle was feeding me. With himself.

The freshness was so good. I was greedy. I swallowed until I could take no more.

"Thanks," I managed to croak.

He didn't answer. Well, not in speaking. He just gave a gentle gurgle. Like a mountain stream trickling over a rock.

He stood up and started to move off. "Don't leave me," I said. "Don't go."

The Wobby Gurgle looked up at the sky. The sun was already rising. I had to get home that night. Another day in the desert would finish me.

And him? Would it finish him too? Where did he live? In a cool burrow somewhere? I didn't know. But I remembered Dad's words. Maybe he stored up water like a camel. Maybe he was carrying twelve years' supply.

I staggered after him, somehow realizing that he was leading me in the right direction. Every now and then he would give a low gurgle, as if to encourage me.

The sun beat down mercilessly. I wondered how he could stand it. My throat was dry. I wanted water. But I didn't like to ask. I knew I would never make it without regular drinks.

7

So did the Wobby Gurgle. He seemed to know when I couldn't go on. Every fifteen minutes or so he would come and put his cool finger into my mouth. And I would feel the trickle of fizzing liquid flowing across my tongue.

He was so gentle. So generous. Waiting. Leading me on. Giving me a drink. Pure, pure water.

After several hours I felt much stronger. But the Wobby Gurgle seemed to be moving more slowly. His steps were shorter. And was it my imagination or had he shrunk?

On we went. On and on. With the cruel sun beating down. We stopped more often for a drink and after each one the Wobby Gurgle walked more slowly.

I looked at him carefully. The tiny fish seemed bigger as it floated effortlessly inside his arm. It wasn't bigger. He was smaller.

I was drinking him.

"No," I screamed. "No. I can't do it. You're killing yourself for me. You'll soon be empty."

He seemed to smile. If a water face can smile.

Once again he placed his finger in my mouth. And like a greedy baby at its mother's breast I sucked and swallowed.

The day wore on and the Wobby Gurgle grew smaller and smaller with every drink. I clamped my jaw shut. I refused to open my mouth. I wasn't going to let him kill himself for me. No way.

114

But it was no use. He simply pointed at my mouth and let fly with a jet of water. It ran down my chin and dripped onto the dry sand, wasted. He wasn't going to stop until I swallowed. I opened my mouth and accepted the gift of life.

As the afternoon wore away, so did the Wobby Gurgle. By now he was only half my size. A little bag of liquid. His steps were small and slow. Like an exhausted child.

I tried to stop him from feeding me. But it was no good. He simply poured himself onto my face if I refused.

In the end he was no bigger than my fist. A small figure, wearily leading me on at a snail's pace. I picked him up in one hand and looked at him. The fish almost totally filled his body. He held no more than a few cupfuls of water.

"That's it," I said. "I'm not taking any more. I'd sooner die myself. If you give me any more I'll run off. You'll never catch me."

He looked up sadly. He knew that he was beaten.

And so was I.

The sun set once again. And the far-off moon, unknowing, uncaring, rose in the night sky.

I thought that I could last until morning. But the tiny Wobby Gurgle, how long could he last?

We both fell asleep. Me and my little friend—the bag of water.

Later I woke and with a fright saw that the Wobby Gurgle was lying on his back, not moving. The dark red fish inside him floated upside down.

"Hey," I yelled, "wake up."

There was no movement. He looked like a tiny, clear football that had been emptied of air. I knew he was dying.

8

Tears trickled down my cheek. How I had enough moisture to make tears I will never know. I was so filled with sorrow that I didn't see the watcher. The sad, silent watcher.

A woman. A water woman. With a gasp I saw her out of the corner of my eye. She seemed to flow across the desert sand rather than walk.

"Quick," I yelled. "Here."

I pointed to the tiny, deflated figure on the sand.

She didn't look at me but just bent over the still figure and gently kissed him on his water lips.

It was the most beautiful sight I had ever seen. Water flowed from her lips into his. She was filling him up. From herself. It was like watching a tire being inflated. He grew larger and she grew smaller. The fish once more began to swim. The kiss of life went on and on until both Wobby Gurgles were the same size. About my size. Three kids in the desert.

Well, no. One kid. And two wonderful half-empty Wobby Gurgles.

They both smiled. So gently. Then the woman held out her water-filled arm and pointed. In the distance I could see a red glow. It was the neon light of the Blue Singlet Motel.

"Thanks," I yelled. It seemed such a small thing to say. I could never repay them for what they had done. I turned around to try and tell them how I felt.

But they had both gone. I was alone in the night.

I walked toward home. As I got closer I could see the police cars. And the search helicopter. Dad would have lots of customers.

But not as many as he would have when the word about the Wobby Gurgles got out.

People made of water.

Visitors would come from everywhere. Australians. Americans. Japanese. Germans. Clicking their cameras. Buying their film. There would be museums. Hotels. Pizza parlors. Probably even slot machines. We would be famous. And rich.

Dad came rushing out with tears streaming down his face. He hugged me until I couldn't breathe.

"How did you stay alive?" he said. "With no water? Did someone help you?"

I looked at him for a long time. The police were listening—everyone wanted to know what had happened. I thought about the Wobby Gurgles. Those shy, generous people. Who had given the water of life to a greedy boy. Then I thought about the crowds with the cameras. And the noise and pizza shops that would follow.

I thought about all the plants and flowers that had vanished from this country forever.

"Well?" said Dad.

He was a good dad. But I knew that he would want to find the Wobby Gurgle.

That's when I looked at him and told a lie.

"No," I said. "I never saw anyone."

Did I do the right thing? You be the judge.